The Independent Bookworm

ABOUT THE BOOK

Once upon a time in a world where magic and technology collide with unexpected consequences…

The cat is caught in a curse with no way out. Not even the death of his hot-tempered owner, the miller, opens an escape route. Instead the youngest of the miller's sons inherits him. Can the cat gain his freedom if he fulfills the boy's unrealizable wish?

What if Charles Perrault hadn't known who or what „Puss in Boots" really was?

ABOUT THE AUTHOR

Ever since she was born, Katharina Gerlach had her head in the clouds. She and her three younger brothers grew up in the middle of a forest in the heart of the Luneburgian Heather. After romping through the forest with imagination as her guide, the tomboy learned to read and disappeared into magical adventures, past times or eerie fairytale woods.

She never returned to Earth for long, although she managed to successfully finish training as a landscape gardener, study forestry and gain a PhD. But then, she discovered her vocation: storytelling and realized she'd have to write to make her dream of sharing her stories with others come true.

Katharina loves to write Fantasy, Science Fiction and Historical Novels for all age groups. At present, she is writing at her next project in a small house near Hildesheim, Germany, where she lives with her husband, three children and a dog.

Mehr Informationen: http://de.KatharinaGerlach.com

THE INHERITANCE

PUSS IN BOOTS
TREASURES RETOLD 10

Katharina Gerlach

The Inheritance, Treasures Retold 10
published by the Independent Bookworm, USA und D
This book is also available as eBook. It has been published in English and in German.

If you find any typos or formatting problems in this eBook, please contact the publisher (www.IndependentBookworm.de).

© 2017, alle Rechte an der Geschichte liegen bei der Autorin

© 2017, cover design by Katharina Kolata, Independent Bookworm

© 2017, title background by Corona Zschusschen, www.sjusjun.com

© 2014, logo by colorgraphix, Guru.com

© 2014, ribbons on logo: Thomas Amby, Shutterstock

© 2017 paragraph divider cat paws: Clker-Free-Vector-Images, Pixabay

© 2017 paragraph divider pea shell: Dim Grits, Hortipendium

editor: Ethan James Clarke, Silverjay Publishing

printed On-Demand Publishing LLC, 100 Enterprise Way, Suite A200, Scotts Valley, CA 95066, USA, www.createspace.com

ISBN-13 978-3-95681-108-1

More Information can be found on the publisher's website:
http://www.IndependentBookworm.de

For my family. I couldn't have done it without you.

TABLE OF CONTENTS

The Inheritance

"I said hares, not rabbits! There isn't enough meat on a rabbit to fill a thimble." The miller's yelling drowned out the singing of the nine-tailed whip as it licked at the tomcat's skin.

Screaming, the cat raced up a beam in the middle of the living room to the rafters where the enraged man couldn't reach him any more. Thankfully the ceilings in the mill's rooms were quite high. The miller had grown fat and lazy from his wealth, and his eldest son was nowhere in sight. The cat sat on a beam and licked the blood off his black fur, hoping the miller would forget the spell. No such luck though. The man practically screamed the command and the cat felt the bond around his throat tighten. Irresistibly, he got pulled back down – and not gently either since he was ripped from his perch. Flying through the air, he managed to turn and land on his paws at the last moment. He hissed, but the whip soon silenced him.

The skin on his left side split open. Bleeding, he managed to crawl beneath the miller's footstool, using what little magic he could muster to make it look like him. With a heavy heart, he felt the power he once possessed just out of reach. Oh how he longed to use it to murder the miller with the slowest and most painful death curse he could find. Instead, he tried to remain as tightly curled under the footstool as he could to avoid the whip's tails.

"Blasted cat." Spittle spilled from the miller's lips and sweat ran from his forehead over his cheeks into his white beard. "That's what I get for feeling you."

"Feeding me?" The cat was enraged, but he kept his voice down. "I don't even get to sleep with all the errands I got to run for you. You do know that that'll be over when you kill me right?"

"Pah!" The miller stopped hitting the footstool and sat in his wingback chair. "My sister made sure you can't be killed so easily."

The cat refrained from telling the miller that creatures like him could not be killed, fullstop. And that was none of the miller's sister's doing. Only the forced labor for a short tempered, cruel human was her fault. He crawled out from under the footstool, took the illusion off it, and began to lick his wounds.

"Don't think you will get away with shoddy work like this." The miller was breathing heavily, maybe even more so than when he was exerting himself, but his face was no longer red. He'd paled considerably. The cat rejoiced. Soon…

"You can't hold me forever," he said quietly. "One day I'll be free, and then I'll take revenge on your whole species."

"Ridiculous. You'll be my servant for as long as I live." The miller's breathing was labored.

"Luckily that won't be all that much longer." The cat curled up on the ground and began to purr.

"I'll live long enough to hand you down to my second son. You will not be free until the day my step-son, the loser, will marry a princess and become heir to the throne." The cat noticed the ties of magic tighten around him. The one loophole in the magical binding he'd watched so carefully ever since his capture eighteen years ago closed just because he couldn't let his tormentor die in peace. He swore silently keeping his gaze fixed on the miller.

The miller sat up straighter but it was a strain, and his breathing grew faster as if he'd run a race. "In other words, you won't be free until hell freezes over. Now, stop staring at me like this and fetch me those hares." He made as if to get up, when the door opened, and his youngest son entered with a bowl of flour in hand.

"Here's the newest grind, father. Father?"

The miller toppled forward.

The bowl dropped to the ground, spilling flour everywhere, as the slender boy tried to support the heavy man. The cat used the chance to get away with a yowl.

"Don't dare to show up without three hares at least," the miller's feeble voice called after him.

Drat, he thought. He'd hoped the dying man would forget about the hares.

🐾 🐾 🐾

Three hours later, the cat still slipped through the underbrush looking for a final hare. He'd caught two young ones in the fields but after their deaths the other hares hid, so he had come to the forest. So far, his luck left him wanting. He was hot and the flour still clung to his underbelly and made his skin itch. Also, the wounds from the whip hurt whenever he touched a branch of fern. *Time for a break,* he thought and turned into the direction of the clearing with the unicorn's pond. Not many people went there any more. He should be safe, at least until his master called for him again. With a sigh, he pushed the last ferns aside and strode into the clearing, tail held high. Even in this body he had a standard to uphold, right?

"Oh, Tom." Two big hands grabbed him around the chest and lifted him off the ground. It was the boy. What did his brothers call him again? Runt. They named him Runt. The youngster held the cat closer to his chest. "I bet Father scared you stiff, the way he toppled and all."

The cat mewed and tried to break free, but his wounds were still too fresh. He couldn't struggle as much as he would have liked to. The boy sat beside the pond, dangling his bare feet into the clear water. He didn't even wet the rim of his pants. They'd grown too small a year ago. Since the miller's wife could no longer protect him (she died), he never got new ones. With gentle fingers he untangled the cat's fur, hesitating when he saw the wounds.

"Again?" He stroked the cat. "I bet you hope he'll die soon." The boy sighed. "Would it shock you to know that I'm wishing for the same? I might be able to get along with Klaus and Oliver, but with Father around I'll be dead before I'm twenty." He held out his skinny arms. "I've got to steal food because he'd rather feed the pigs than give the leftovers to me."

Under the gentle stroking, the cat couldn't help but purr. He didn't care much for the boy's woes but that didn't seem to bother Runt. Vaguely, the cat seemed to remember that there used to be a different name back when the miller's wife was still alive. Oh, how well they'd eaten back then. He purred louder, and Runt laughed.

"At least you're feeling better now," he said. "I wish I'd find an easy remedy like that." He sat the cat aside. "Sorry, but I got to go now. Klaus told me to fetch water from this pond for Father. It's said to have healing power."

Only now did the cat notice the mug in the grass beside the boy. Under no circumstances could he allow the miller to have water from a unicorn's pond.

Lengthening his life like that simply wouldn't do. He needed a plan. To buy some time, he lapped up some of the water carefully and enjoyed the sensation of his skin healing in record time. When the boy knelt down to fill his mug, the cat extended his claws and dragged them over his fingers.

"Ouch!" With the mug tumbling into the water, Runt sat back and stared at him in surprise. "What was that for?"

The cat mewed again, lifted his tail, and walked away. The lake's bank was steep here which meant Runt would have to go diving. That'd do him good and prevent an infection of the scratches. For a fleeting moment, the cat felt a little guilty. Runt had never been anything but friendly to him. But he needed the delay to find a solution for the problem. The miller could not have water from a unicorn's pond even if it was far less potent now than at night, when the unicorn refilled the magic. At least the beautiful creature was still free. He could feel its magic somewhere close. Unlike him, it would have died in captivity.

"But it must be around here." A bright voice rang through the forest. "We followed the directions to the dot."

"Maybe we should have taken the kitchen maid along after all," a second voice suggested.

The cat crouched into the ferns to hide but peeked out at the two girls walking between the trees with a big basket carried between the two of them. Its contents smelled delicious.

"How am I supposed to catch a husband with more freckles than a quail's egg." The bigger girl looked around in agitation.

The dainty one sighed. "I keep telling you that it doesn't matter. A man who's in love with you will love your freckles too, Margot."

"That may be the case, Your Highness. But I want that pond." The girl called Margot pulled her companion to the right, which incidentally was the right direction. Intrigued, the cat followed them, remaining invisible behind ferns and bushes. Maybe they could be turned into a solution for his problem. After all both were young and, considering human standards, kind of beautiful despite the drab clothing, and Runt had the right age to appreciate that. It was something the cat could work with.

"There it is!" The bigger girl stopped and sat down the basket. "See, I told you it'd be around here."

"Yes, Margot. Can we leave now?"

"My dear Princess Felicitas. We came here to bathe my skin, and bathe I will."

"But there's a man over there." The petite brunette nodded to the other side of the pond where the boy stood open-mouthed and motionless, mug in hand.

A princess! The cat's heart began to pound. If that's true, her worn garments must be a disguise. The possible solution to his current problem might yet prove to be the miller's undoing.

Margot sighed. "Hello, young man? Yes, you there. Would you have the decency to go away? I'm going to bathe now."

The young man didn't move. Despite the water running from his hair and clothes, he seemed frozen in place. The cat sneered. It was just the reaction he had expected from the boy. He pulled his magic into him. Here at the unicorn's pond, it was stronger than at the mill. He created the illusion of a tentacle lifting itself from the water. At the same time, he called up a strong wind which pushed at the girls. Margot screamed as if she was going to die and dove to the ground, but the princess pulled something from the pocket of her well-mended skirt and just stared at the tentacle. The illusion grabbed her, and she swung her knife in a circle. It sliced through the illusion without effect, and she toppled into the water, pushed by the wind the cat focused on her.

"She'll drown!" Margot screamed at the top of her lungs. "She can't swim."

The cat purred silently. His plan seemed to work. When the boy dropped the mug he had obviously just recovered and jumped into the water again, he ran from his hiding place. Time to fill the mug with non-magical water from the nearby stream.

Where on Earth did that tentacle come from? Alexander was in the water before his brain finished formulating that question. In no time, he reached the girl whose beauty had mesmerized him just a second ago. It wasn't a very big pond, and he was fast, and the girl clearly needed saving. She was thrashing around like a drowning cat, and her eyes showed a lot of white. Despite her terror, she didn't scream though. Alexander marveled at her guts as he reached for her shoulders.

"Ouch!"

Her hand had connected with his nose. He must get behind her or they'd both drown. Taking a deep breath, he dove and swam around her under water. When he came up again, he was in her back. As fast as he could, he grabbed her under her shoulders and began to swim backwards, using his legs abd dragging her along. First she kept struggling but soon she relaxed a little. Maybe she had realized he was holding her. Would she allow him to kiss her hand when they were on land again?

Before they reached the pond's steep bank, his question caught up with him again. Where exactly had the tentacle come from? He'd been swimming in the pond often without ever encountering anything with tentacles before. And whatever creature it belonged to had not tried to eat the girl or him. After successfully getting the girl into the water it had vanished as if it had never been.

He pushed the girl close enough to the bank that she could stand. "It's getting less steep here," he said, helped her to her feet and out of the water. Dripping, he followed her. The other girl sat up and stared at him as if he came from another world. Behind her, Alexander caught a glimpse of his step-father's black tomcat with the white star on his forehead. Could it have been the tom's work? Nonsense. Who had ever heard of a cat doing magic. He turned toward the girls again and bowed deeply.

"I do not know where that tentacle came from," he said, "but I can assure you that there's no tentacled creature in this pond. Maybe it was a magical illusion."

"That makes sense." The bigger girl's eyes narrowed. "Kidnapping would be easy here. Maybe you wanted to capture the pr…"

"Margot!" The brunette girl hit her friend on the arm hard enough to make her wince before she turned to Alexander. "I am grateful for your help. I really am. Are you sure there's no strange creature?"

"I've swum here many times without encountering anything like it." He smiled as best he could without giving away how wobbly his knees were. After all, the girl's dress was clinging to her body rather suggestively. He tried not to stare. "And I know for sure that the pond's owner clears it from vermin every night. I watched it a couple of times."

"So it could well have been magic." The brunette stopped squeezing water from her dress and hair and held out a hand. "I'm Felicitas. Thank you for rescuing me."

All of a sudden, Alexander's heart seemed to have jumped into his throat. "My name's Alexander," he croaked, took the offered hand, bent over, and blew a kiss on the dainty fingers before he let them go again. "But my brothers call me Runt."

The petite brunette giggled.

"Oh, an old-fashioned cavalier." The second girl stood up. "Let's go home, Felicitas."

"But I thought you wanted to bathe in the water."

"Not with some unknown creature in its depth." Margot remained adamant. "I'd rather live and die with freckles than getting snatched up by a monster or worse a witch or enchanter who can conjure monsters. Thank you."

"Oh, Margot. You should see your face so full of disdain." Felicitas laughed out loud. "Let's have the picnic at least before we leave." The dripping girl turned to Alexander. "Would you care to eat with us? I'd be delighted to get to know my savior a little better."

Alexander blushed, cursing his skinny body. With his shirt wet one could see every little muscle and even his ribs. Surely the girl thought he could do with a little food. He bowed again to hide his embarrassment. "I'd be delighted to keep you company, but there's no need to share your food with me. I will eat when I am home."

"Nonsense. There's enough for a whole army in the basket." Felicitas didn't budge, and so Alexander found himself sitting on a striped blanket with the girls only a few minutes later. The smell of the dishes alone made him feel dizzy. His stomach grumbled. He clenched his fists glancing at the girls, but neither seemed to have noticed.

"Why are your brothers calling you Runt?" Felicitas handed him a plate loaded with sandwiches, eggs, meat, and carrots. "It's not a very nice name."

"I am the most delicate of us three. When Mother still lived, she always worried about me the most, and the others were quite jealous about it." Alexander had to force himself not to swallow the food in one bite.

"And why did you come to the pond today?" Felicitas' smile made his heart stumble.

Alexander's mouth went dry. How could a mere girl have such an effect on him. He took a sip from the cup they had filled for him before he answered. "The miller, I mean Father, is ill and needs water from the pond."

"Oh, I'm sorry to hear that." The girl cocked her head and smiled some more. "How lucky for me though that you didn't have to work with your brothers."

"It's not bad working with them. At least they don't … I mean, they're friendly enough as long as I do my share of the work. There's always a lot of work at the mill." Glad that he could change the subject, he began to tell them all about life in a mill and was surprised to find that Felicitas asked intelligent and interested questions. The food diminished in no time. Soon, all the plates were empty, but Felicitas and Alexander had

20

yet to run out of words. He felt as if he'd been waiting for a person like Felicitas to talk to for his entire life.

"Living in a mill seems like fun." Felicitas voice sounded wistful.

"Most of all it is a lot of work," he said.

"I don't mind hard, honest work. It's better than sitting around, doing nothing, waiting for a suitor that pleases your father."

"At least you will get suitors," Margot said. "With my freckles everyone excuses themselves after the first glimpse."

Alexander's eyebrows rose. "I think you are a very beautiful woman, especially with freckles. Most girls in the village have them."

Margot snorted. "I'm not some peasant girl. I'm supposed to have a pale, flawless complexion. If only I could have gone swimming in the pond."

Felicitas' grin held a wicked edge. "In that case you'll probably have to find a witch. She might be able to change the way you look."

"I wouldn't rely on a witch," Alexander said. "Their price is hardly ever worth their remedy. Why don't you take a pitcher of the pond's water with you? If you wash your face in it every morning, the freckles will diminish."

"It's worth a try." Margot filled both wine bottles with water from the pond while Felicitas packed the remains of the food back into the hamper.

Alexander's gaze fell on his mug with water standing lonely in the grass, and he paled. "Oh dear, I completely forgot about Father. I must run."

Felicitas put her hand on his arm as he was trying to get up. "Will you be here again some time soon? I'd like to see you again if you can free yourself from your duties."

Warmth spread from her fingers through Alexander's body and he couldn't help but smile down at her. It was so hard not to bend forward and kiss those lips … the soft, rosy lips under the slender nose and the wide, doe-like eyes. Suddenly his voice sounded strained. "I often come here in the evenings and on Sundays." Those lips. He had to get away before he did something stupid. A girl like her would remain out of his limits forever. He bowed as best he could and got up. "I've really got to hurry now. My father is waiting for the water."

Before Felicitas could say another word, he sprinted to where he left his water, picked up the mug, and hurried away through the bushes.

"Not the most polite man, wasn't he." Margot's voice rang through the forest as if it was hunting him. Felicitas' reply was lost in the rustling of the leaves under his feet.

He could see his oldest brother waiting at the mill's door from afar. His impatiently tapping foot told him that he was in trouble. Expecting at least a cuff around the ears, he held out the mug.

"You daydreaming buffoon," Klaus said. "I'll never understand why mother took you in, foundling. You've only caused problems. Let's just hope the water will still be on time." He grabbed the mug and walked through the mill, up the stairs to his step-father's bedroom.

Alexander followed him. He had to. A sense of foreboding drove him on. He was sure he'd never see Felicitas again if he didn't visit his step-father.

"Here's the water from the unicorn's pond," Klaus said and knelt at his father's side.

"You took your time about it, didn't you?"

Alexander had never heard his step-father's voice so weak.

"It's Runt's fault."

"It always is." The sick man tried to sit up after draining the mug. Klaus helped him, stuffing cushions in his back to stop him from toppling over. The miller's voice grew a little stronger. "Fetch Olli."

It wasn't clear whom he was talking to, so Alexander stayed although he knew fully well that he was the only one ordered around in that tone in this family. Luckily the door opened at that moment, admitting the miller's second son, Oliver. On his heels came the tom, but aside from Alexander no one seemed to notice.

"Aunt Theophelia is on her way," Oliver announced. "She told me to let you know. The old hag is probably looking forward to see you die, old man."

"He won't die. He drank water from the unicorn's pond." Klaus stood up and balled his hands to fists the size of the smith's biggest hammer.

Oliver laughed. It was a hard sound that hurt Alexander's ears. "As if that'd help. One needs to have a pure heart for it to pull one back from the brink of death."

"How come you're here before her?" Klaus obviously made a conscious effort to relax his hands but they opened and closed as if they longed to close around his brother's neck.

"I mastered the art of instant travel, and she thought it good practice." Oliver walked to the other side of his father's bed and sat down on the rim. "Tell me you're proud of me, Father. Hurry before the hag's here. She doesn't like me getting praised. But I'll make her praise me as soon as I know all her spells. My magic's much stronger than hers. She said so."

"Just remember to protect the mill and your brother." The old miller lay with his eyes closed, breathing heavily. "If both of you survive your Aunt, I'll be proud of you."

"But you won't be able to tell me then." Oliver glared at his father. "You're dying."

The cat watched the people in the room from below the miller's footstool. The tension in the room was noticeable. Runt cowered in a corner beside the door, and the two brothers glared at each other while the miller fought for every breath. The cat's heart hammered in anticipation. If the man died without speaking out his will, the spell that bound him to this body would crumble, and he'd be free to take revenge on the puny humans.

A black flower-shaped shadow appeared in the air at the end of the bed. It widened and coalesced into the form of a beautiful woman. Her raven hair fell like a dark waterfall over her bare shoulders; the skirt of her black silken dress filled the room from the bed to the door. Smoky, black tendrils reached from her hair to the dying man on the bed; clearly black magic. The cat wondered why he'd never noticed them before.

"I knew you'd come," said the miller.

"I knew you'd live long enough," his sister retorted.

"Hear my will then. I'm leaving the mill, my lands, the house in town, and everything that goes with it to Klaus, my eldest son." The cat could see the toll the words were having on the miller. Beads of sweat rolled over his face and he was paler than curd cheese. "The cat will go to…"

"Just a moment," his sister interrupted. "Before you pass on the cat, remember that you owe me your soul for it still. It was part of the bargain."

"You can't have it." The miller's eyes sparkled with anger, and a sudden burst of energy made him sit up. The cat rejoiced; it could feel the man's remaining strength ebb away fast.

"The only way out of the bargain is to pass the payment and everything connected to it on with the cat." The woman smiled a smile so cold, it froze the cat to the marrow. If he'd ever encountered an evil witch it was the miller's sister.

With a sigh, the miller sank back into his cushions. The cat knew he'd only had a few more minutes to live, and the miller seemed to sense it too. "Klaus, you will share your wealth fifty-fifty with your brother Oliver for as long as he protects you and the mill. I am leaving the cat and all the restrictions of his labor including the payment I owe my sister to my step-son Alexander."

The witch and the miller's sons screamed in rage while the black threads tied to the miller unraveled and merged with the boy's hair. The new connection with the witch made it absolutely clear to the cat that the curse had accepted the dying man's words. He hissed. *Drat. Couldn't the man have died one minute earlier? At least I won't have to talk to the boy. I'll simply pretend I'm a normal cat, and he'll soon lose interest in me.* Then he noticed that the miller was still speaking. The dying man's voice rang over the din like a churchbell, and only the cat knew that it was due to the spell whose last loophole the miller was now changing.

"If my step-son marries a princess and becomes heir to a kingdom, the cat will be free and the payment forfeit." The room fell silent so the miller's croaky chuckle could be heard. "And that will never come to pass."

"You idiot. How can you allow him a way out?" The witch raised her arms and began to speak in a strange language. The cat felt a surge of magic grabbing his bonds, strengthening them tenfold when the witch added yet another condition to his freedom.

"He will only be free over my dead body," she said. "For only if the price of a soul has been paid shall his ties crumble."

The black magic bonds around the cat tightened even more. He could barely breathe. But before he blacked out, he noticed with great satisfaction that the miller gasped and fell back open mouthed, no longer breathing.

The late miller's oldest set of black clothes, hung from Alexander like a shroud as he sat on the mill's steps and stroked the black tom on his lap. It still hadn't recovered fully from whatever the witch's magic had done to it. Most of the time it stared unseeing into the air. He felt sorry for the animal and wondered why the dying man and his sister had been so adamant about a cat's freedom. And what that about a soul as payment? Payment for what? And why did a cat have to be paid? For a fleeting moment, he wondered if his soul was in danger, now that the miller had left him the cat and the payment, but a cuff to his ears stopped his musing.

"Hurry, the service will start punctually." Klaus walked past him. Obediently, Alexander jumped to his feet and followed his brother to the horse drawn cart with the black bows that would take them and the miller's coffin to the village's church. For reasons unknown, Oliver disliked the modern steam engine vehicles, so the miller had never bought one. From his seat in the back, Alexander watched the cat grow smaller and smaller the further they drove, and his thoughts returned to his own predicament.

Of course, the miller hadn't been nice but at least he had felt the obligation to house him and occasionally even feed him. Alexander was sure that his step-brothers wouldn't hesitate a second if they saw a chance to earn some money with him. And the recruiting teams from some of the neighboring kingdoms didn't care whom they paid for as long as they fulfilled their quota. He might find himself bound to an army and shipped off to a place at war that he'd never seen and would never have traveled to of his own free will. And that would mean he'd never see Felicitas again. He sat through the service and paid his respects at the grave, feeling numb inside, trying to find a solution for his pending doom.

His only option was to leave before the miller's sons found a way to get rid of him. If only he had a place to go to. As a vagabond no one would employ him, and without work he'd starve. He'd seen the hopeless when they passed the mill by after his step-mother's death because they knew they were no longer welcome there. The hunger on their faces had cut his heart each time. He didn't want to end like that.

"Feed the horses and then head home and clean out father's room," Klaus ordered as the participants of the service entered the inn beside the church for the customary Departion Meal. "We can't be seen with the likes of you."

Alexander obeyed wordlessly. The horses were tied to a wooden bar near the church and couldn't graze, so he fetched them the hey they had brought along on the cart. His brothers would stay at the inn for quite a while. They both enjoyed a good drink and the company of respected farmers. With a sigh, Alexander set out to their mill.

When he reached it, his feet hurt. The tom was still sitting in the same place as it had when they left. He kneeled to stroke it. Poor old tom. I'm sure they'll chuck you out too as soon as they're back. After all, you're mine now, and you never caught many mice anyway.

The cat sat motionless like a statue. Something had most definitely happened to it when the miller died. Alexander didn't like the far-away look in its eyes one bit. Had the witch cursed the animal? But why would she do that? It was only a cat. Alexander tried to cheer him up, at least a little.

"You know what? I might not be able to give you much, but you should have a name." He put his hand on the tom's head. "I hereby name you Hunter."

The cat's gaze returned from whatever place it had watched. He cocked his head and purred a little. Then he got up and took a step toward the woods.

"You're right. We should be leaving of our own accord, but where will I go?" It felt good to voice his fears even if it was only a cat listening. "Vagabonds don't get jobs because they can't give a home address, and those are required these days. And if I don't get a job, I won't be able to get a Card of Residency which would allow me to rent a room somewhere in the kingdom. Whatever I do, I'll have no chance."

"Miaowww." Hunter took another step.

Alexander sighed. Maybe the tom was right. It'd be better to live as a vagabond than to die pressed into the army of a country he didn't care for. "I'll fetch my things. Wait for me, please."

To his surprise, the tom sat down again as if he had understood.

It didn't take Alexander long to pack the few belongings he had, his old clothes (even though they were too small they could still be used), a threadbare blanket, the pocket knife his step-mother had gifted him years ago, a loaf of bread (he felt entitled to it after all the unpaid work he'd done over the years), and the locket on the brass chain he had worn as a baby when the miller's wife had found him. Luckily she had never told her husband about it, or it would have been long gone. He hung it around his neck and tucked it under the miller's old shirt.

When he exited the mill, Hunter was still waiting for him. As soon as he set eyes on Alexander, he resumed his walk to the woods. They left the mill's grounds through the garden, and all of a sudden, Alexander felt as if a heavy burden had been lifted from his shoulders. Regardless how hard his life would become, from now on no one would slap him around any more. He didn't even notice that he walked straighter and with a spring in his step.

🐾 🐾 🐾

Hunter observed the boy as he led him through the forest. He must be more attuned to the magical world than he had thought possible. Why else had he named him – and very appropriately? The boy was a riddle. There was something about him that Hunter couldn't put his paw on.

He doesn't seem to be aware that he might have strange abilities, he thought. *I have to tread carefully. I wonder what will happen when the witch comes to collect his soul. Should I train him in magic so he can defeat her? She said I'd be free 'over her dead body only'.* Hunter sighed when he remembered the second half of the binding. It seemed impossible to get the boy to marry the princess. *Although he's handsome enough.* His musings went into the new direction. *The king would probably approve of him if only he'd been born noble. The princess is no problem at all. She certainly likes him already. Now, what can I do to even the odds a little?*

Lost in thought he led the boy – he'd decided to stop calling him Runt, it no longer fit him – to the unicorn's pond. It was a good place for a home base. As a first step he had to teach the boy, without talking, how to survive in the wild while he found a way how the boy could marry the princess. Not exactly easy tasks, especially since his senses hadn't fully recovered yet. Scents were muddy, his vision a lot less accurate than normal, and all he could hear were the birds in the trees and the boy's footsteps. Therefore, he was just as surprised as the boy when they broke through the bushes at the pond and found Felicitas sitting at its rim.

She jumped to her feet and blushed. "Oh, hello. I … I didn't think you'd come here again this soon."

"I am sorry for my intrusion. I will leave." The boy bowed stiffly and turned to go, but the girl stopped him.

"That's not what I meant." She came over and crouched to stroke Hunter. Reluctantly he allowed his animal instinct to take over. Purring might be the least conspicuous thing to do for him right now, so he listened to the girl. "I came here to sort out some problems I have and just didn't expect to see anyone here today. I'm delighted that you're here though. I really enjoyed our talk last week."

Hunter could smell how pleased the boy was. He turned on his back, drawing the princess' gaze away from his new master's blushing face.

"So what are you doing here today? Does your father need another dose of the water?" She looked up at the boy.

"He wasn't my real father." Sweat built up on the boy's forehead.

Hunter snorted with annoyance. Couldn't he speak to a beautiful girl without making a fool of himself? He did it well enough the other day.

"I left home to find my fortune." The boy's voice wobbled, so the cat meowed to draw the princess' attention. He needed her to fall in love with the boy. After all, they had to get married or he'd never be free. Although how he would get the king to approve of a marriage between a commoner and his daughter, Hunter didn't yet know. But where there was a will, there would be a way.

"Why don't you work in the castle kitchen?" The princess rubbed Hunter's belly and didn't look up. Amused, he noticed that she was blushing too. And she rattled on. "The king is a gourmet, and his cooks are always looking for help since most servants run away after a while. They are not used to working so hard. But you look as if you wouldn't mind that. I mean, toiling at a mill you are surely strong enough, aren't you?"

"I never worked in a kitchen, but I could give it a try." A first tentative smile tucked at the corners of the boy's mouth. He sat in the grass beside the princess and began to scratch Hunter's ears. "What would I have to do?"

The princess explained, and Hunter wondered how she learned so much about cooking. It was not usually part of a princess' education. Could it be possible that she wasn't the kingdom's princess after all? Maybe she really was the scullery maid she had pretended to be. But then he remembered the other woman. She had certainly called her by her title. Felicitas had to be the king's daughter.

"Well, it doesn't sound too bad," the boy said. "I think I should be able to manage that."

"In that case, I'm going to give you an advance." The girl pulled a silver coin from her pocket and pressed it into the boy's hand dismissing his protest. "Stop fussing. The head cook will refund it. You'd better concentrate on the work ahead of you. As I said, the worst task you could get is the plucking of birds. My father is especially fond of partridge. They've been hunted to extinction in the Royal Hunting Grounds."

Hunter rejoiced. Now he knew for sure that he'd been right to facilitate the bonding of the two. And the mentioning of partridge had already triggered a few ideas.

"Your father?" The boy sat back with eyes as big as saucers. His voice trembled as he asked, "You're the king's daughter?"

"No ... I mean, yes, but I ... I didn't ... I wasn't trying to deceive you. "There were tears in the princess' eyes. "It's just so rare that I can simply talk to someone without them bowing, bootlicking or currying favors."

"You're the princess." The boy stumbled to his feet and bowed. "I'm very sorry for being so ... so ... I'm a simpleton, like my brothers said."

The princess got to her feet to and held out her hands toward the boy, but he retreated. She let her arm sink. When she spoke, her voice sounded choked. "I'm sorry that I didn't tell you right away. It's been such a pleasure talking to you. If only we could ... never mind. I'm fated to marry the prince from three kingdoms over anyway."

"The War Prince?"

"The same. Father has no choice. Either I marry the prince, or our country is facing a war." Her smile was sad. "For now, he's hiding behind his banquets, but he doesn't have much time left. I'm sorry, Alexander. I never meant to deceive you."

The boy – Alexander, Hunter reminded himself – drew several deep breaths, then straightened. He bent forward a little and looked the princess into the eyes.

"I am not sorry." He seemed to have mastered his shock. To Hunter it seemed as if he'd even gained some guts. His words were strong and full of emotion. "Even though we'll never see each other again, the time with you will be my most treasured memory. But you must go now."

"I don't want to." The princess stepped closer to Alexander and put her delicate hand on the lapel of his jacket. It resembled a pale flower. She lifted her face with a sad smile. Then, without warning, she stood on her toes, kissed him, turned, and ran. Alexander stared after her as if he'd seen a ghost. She was long gone before his hand slowly rose to his lips. He sighed.

"Well, that went a lot better than I could have hoped for," Hunter said. "And I haven't even begun planning yet."

Alexander nearly jumped out of his skin when he heard his cat talk, sadness replaced by shock. Panting, with both hands pressed to his chest, he tried to wrap his head around the miracle. "You ... you ... can talk?"

"Naturally." The tom preened himself. "I just do not talk to everyone and their cousin."

"But..." Alexander's mind still reeled. His legs wobbled as if made from unbaked bread dough, so he sat in the grass. Well, if the forest contained unicorns, why not a talking cat. He wondered how the miller, he no longer thought of him as his step-father, had managed to lure the creature into his service. Realization dawned. "You were a slave as much as I were."

"You named me, so you're my responsibility now." Hunter curled his tail around his legs. "Am I assuming right that you fancy Princess Felicitas? Would you like to marry her?"

Alexander didn't know what to say. In his chest hope and longing battled common sense. Would a magical tomcat really be able to help him gain not only the princess' love but also her hand in marriage? "But what about the threat of war?"

"Let's take one step after the other." Hunter cocked his head. "First we'll need to convince the king that you're worthy of his only child, and that'll be hard enough."

"He'll never like me." Alexander wiped his eyes. "How can he? I'm not of noble lineage, and not even presentable."

"The first step is to impress him, and I know exactly how to do that." Hunter got up and walked toward Alexander on his hind legs. He stretched the rear paws a couple of times and winced. "These legs are not really made for walking upright, but I think I can manage. I need boots – red – and a few clothes. Also, I need an old sack and a little bit of grain. The coin the princess gave you should be enough for all of this."

"But it's all the money I have. I could live on it for weeks," Alexander protested.

"Felicitas hired you as a sub-cook. If I don't produce results two days after the clothes are done, I'll personally accompany you to the royal kitchen. You'll be able to earn enough money then." Hunter touched Alexander's hand with his front paw. "Come on. If we hurry we'll reach the city in the borderlands by nightfall tomorrow."

Reluctantly Alexander got up. "Why don't we go to the capital? It's much closer."

"We can't risk anyone from the castle seeing you." Hunter strode past him as fast as his short hind legs would carry him. "Come on."

When they left the woods, Hunter felt the tingle of magic on his pawtips. He might not be able to use much of it, but it was still more than he had at his disposal for the last twenty-odd years. He felt like purring.

They reached the town just before they were closing the gates. Naturally the guards were reluctant to let in someone in a dress at least two sizes too wide but one size too short.

"We don't allow vagabonds," the older one said.

Before Alexander could answer, Hunter spoke: "Count duMas and I are no vagabonds. We simply travel incognito. Now, let us past, you imbecile."

The two guards stared at him much like Alexander had earlier.

"A talking cat?" The older soldier scratched his head.

"Do you think, Count duMas would accept any old servant?" Hunter glared at the soldier. A pleasurable shiver ran down his spine. Humans were so ... easy to impress. It was despicable. Using a tiny drop of magic and his paw, he pushed against one guard's thigh, and the man flew through the air like a rag doll. Alexander gasped, ran to where he had landed with a thud and reached out to help him to his feet.

"Please forgive my friend." He glared at Hunter. "He's sometimes a little intemperate."

The guard scrambled backward. "Get away from me."

The second guard lowered his lance. "Leave him alone, or I'll run you through."

"Hunter! "Alexander's voice cut through the cat's body like a hit with a whip. The well known pain of disobedience raced through his body. When Alexander spoke again, his voice sounded friendlier, but firm. "Now look what you've done. I want you to apologize."

The command sucked away the little bit of magic Hunter had been able to gather. He hissed.

"Now!" Alexander's voice made it clear that he wouldn't take a no for a no.

Hunter wondered if he had misjudged the boy. But command was command. He took a few steps toward the guard and bowed. "I am terribly sorry for this inconvenience. I sometimes forget my own strength. It wasn't my intention to hurt you."

The guard, now back on his feet, waved him away. "Find yourselves an inn. If I hear of another 'accident' of this kind, I'll put you both in jail and throw away the key."

Hunter knew when he was no longer wanted, so he took his leave. To his relief, Alexander followed him swiftly.

"Why did you do that?" The furrowed brow told Hunter that the boy was still angry. "The guards were no threat. Why did you attack?"

Hunter didn't answer. With somnambulistic confidence he found the cobbler's shop. The master was just in the process of closing for the night. With a sigh, Alexander ordered boots made of red leather from him. Hunter wanted to take him to a hat maker and a tailor next, but all shops were closed.

So he found a box of old clothes in a side street where his master could sleep, and made sure that not even rats would disturb his slumber while he fumed about the fact that he was still bound to a human. How much longer would it take to gain his freedom? He longed to rip out the witch's heart and force Alexander to eat it until he choked on it. Not that he hated the boy, but he was his master after all. Therefore, he had to be punished. On principle alone. And then he'd kill the miller's biological sons, especially the witch's apprentice. Oh, it'd be so much fun to show him how little he knew of magic. Maybe he'd also kill a few other humans, just to show them who had the real power.

But I won't touch the princess, he thought. *She's been nice to me whenever we met.*

The next morning, Alexander woke with a sore back. He counted the change wondering if there'd be enough left by the end of the day to buy some food.

Still, he followed Hunter to a tailor silently and paid for a black cloak with green velvet lining. After the next stop, a hat maker where he ordered and paid for a green hat with a white feather, he had only a few coppers left. His stomach grumbled. He glanced at his cat who was walking – still upright – toward a tiny patch of grass with trees in the middle of the town. The inhabitants had called it a 'park', and Hunter had suggested they'd wait there since all the craftsmen had promised to be done by nightfall. To reach it, they had to walk through the market. It was quite difficult to stay near the cat. He was far more agile and avoided the clusters of buyers and sellers with a natural grace Alexander envied.

When they passed a stall with fish, he noticed Hunter's tongue shooting out. It licked over the cat's lips and vanished again. Alexander realized that he'd never seen him eat. The miller had never fed him and, as far as he could remember, neither had the miller's sons. The coins in his hand burned. Abruptly he stopped at the stall and asked, "I've got three coppers. How much fish can you give me for that?"

"Depends on the quality. The seller seemed tight-lipped. Filet – none. Rests – half a bag."

"I'll take the rests then." Alexander handed over his money. It hurt to see it go, but if Hunter was really able to find a way how he could see Felicitas again, this was a small sacrifice to make. With a small bag made of oiled paper he hurried to the park, looking for Hunter. He found the cat sitting on the grass beside a bush. With a slightly crooked smile, he held out the bag. "For you."

The cat's eyes grew wide and wider. His mouth opened and closed but not a single word came out. Still, he didn't take the bag. After a while he swallowed and cleared his throat.

"You do know that a gift for me means you can't order me around any longer, right?"

"Sorry?" Alexander didn't know what Hunter was talking about.

"I'd still be bound to you, but you couldn't make me obey your commands like you did yesterday when you forced me to apologize." Hunter's eyes glowed like little torches.

"You only obeyed my request because you had to?" Alexander was taken aback. "I thought you did so because you're a decent person – cat – whatever. I'd never treat anyone like a slave." He pressed the bag with the fish in Hunter's paw to make him understand the truth of his words. "Not you, not anyone else. Not even if it were the miller or his sons. No one deserves that fate."

"Oh …" The furrow between Hunter's brows vanished, and he looked confused. After a time of silence where he studied Alexander with twitching features the young man couldn't interpret, he opened the bag and began to eat. Half way through the bag, he held it out to Alexander. "Want some?"

Hunters emotions were in turmoil, but he was glad Alexander had declined the fish. It'd been so long since he had any that even the leftovers tasted like heaven. Why had the boy – why had Alexander done that? Did he really mean what he had said? Was it possible that some humans weren't greedy, needing, only thinking of themselves, or was Alexander the only one? Hunter thought of the princess and how readily she had shared her food with the dripping young man in threadbare clothes. Could he be wrong? He ate in silence, but watched Alexander from the corners of his eyes. The young man pulled the stale loaf of bread from his bundle, unwrapped it, and broke off a small piece before returning the rest to his bundle again. Then, he nibbled on the hard crust as if he wasn't hungry, but Hunter could hear his stomach complain. What a strange boy – man, he reminded himself, Alexander was a man, a young one but nonetheless a man. Were there more people like him?

Hunter decided to find out. He curled up and buried his head under his tail, knowing that he'd look asleep for everyone. Carefully he gathered whatever magic was still floating around. It wasn't much, the kingdom was too technically advanced for that, but it would be enough for the experiment he had in mind. With an inaudible yell of elation, he catapulted himself out of his body. It felt so good to be finally free enough to do that again. Now, if only he could regain his full magical abilities ...

For a little while, he watched Alexander. The young man seemed to enjoy the park. When a little girl fell and hurt her knee not far from him, he went over and comforted her until the knee stopped bleeding and she was smiling again.

Hunter followed the girl. She ran to a male adult, hugged him, and told him everything about her accident. Smiling, the man took her hand and walked toward the market to buy her some sweets. Another man bumped into him.

"Don't worry, nothing happened," he said when the other man apologized profoundly. The girl's father kept smiling although Hunter sensed his annoyance. He also saw the other man's hand slip a purse that wasn't his into a hidden pocket of his coat.

"Daddy is gong to buy me some sweets, you know?" The girl pointed to her sore knee. "I had an accident too. If you're hurt, I'll share my sweets with you."

The pickpocket smiled, patted the girl's hair and her father's shoulder, and walked away. Only Hunter saw that he'd slipped the purse back into his victim's pocket.

It's spreading. Hunter was intrigued. *Alexander's friendliness seems to be contagious.*

For the rest of the day he kept following people around to see how far the spreading went. He soon discovered that there were far more people trying to be nice than people intrinsically bad tempered and grumpy. Slowly his view of humanity shifted. When the magic ran out and he was forced to return to his body, he pondered if he really had to kill the miller's family. Maybe Alexander could infect them with friendliness too. He opened his eyes.

"It's time", he said. "Let's fetch my things and start a little hunt in the woods."

Dawn was already on its way when Hunter and Alexander reached the rim of a forest not too far from the capital where the scent of partridge was strong. Obviously the king's hunting hadn't really driven the birds to extinction. It had just made them more secretive which wouldn't help them when a cat was on the hunt.

"We'll rest here," he said.

The young man sank to the ground with a sigh of relief which reminded Hunter a little late that humans weren't as hardy as cats. He'd have to keep that in mind the next time they traveled.

While Alexander rested, Hunter set up his traps, grains on the ground with nooses. Then he settled down beside his master and curled up. Just before he drifted off to sleep, one of his drowsy thoughts insisted that lying beside the warm body of a human was extremely nice, and so he purred.

When he woke, Alexander was trying to light a fire without success. He was dripping wet.

"What did you do?" Hunter glared at the pool of water at the young man's feet, took a step back, flicked his tail and the dry branches Alexander had collected burst into flame.

"I caught breakfast." He picked up a big trout he'd already gutted and stuck a sapling through it that he'd cut off. "You seemed to like fish: I just didn't expect it to be so hard to catch."

"I'll check the traps." Hunter left, wondering why his heart felt as if someone had tied a knot in it. Obviously Alexander had decided to feed him properly, so why did it cause these strange feelings?

In the five traps he'd set up, he found three partridges. The two females were already dead, the cock too weak to fight when her killed him. A pang of sadness made his whiskers twitch, but nature worked that way, eat or be eaten. At least the birds didn't feed chicks at this time of the year. He put the corpses into the sack Alexander had fished from a pile of waste near the town and returned to the fire. The fish smelled deliciously. His stomach grumbled and eh could barely wait for Alexander to share. His master had undressed and hung his clothes over young trees and branches that hung close to the fire. Steaming puddles showed that they were already drying.

After breakfast, Hunter licked himself clean before explaining a little bit of his plan. "It's not far to the castle. I'll take the birds there while you wait here."

"If the goal is to impress the king, shouldn't I be the one taking them?"

"Do you really think the guards would let in someone in a bedraggled suit that's too big? Why do you think I insisted on the boots, hat and coat?" Hunter put on his new finery. "Not only has the Court never heard a cat talk, they've never seen one this fashionable either, and most likely never will again."

"If you think that'll help." Alexander's smile was weak and insecure. "I'll stay here to dry my clothes then. And afterwards, I'll return to the unicorn's pond."

It took Hunter longer than he had thought to carry the sack into town and up the steep hill to the king's castle. The dead animals proved to be heavy for his cat's body, so he needed several breaks. He reached the castle's main entrance some time after lunch. Well, the birds would still be fine for dinner. Shifting the sack form one shoulder to the other, he approached the guards and announced, "In the name of my master, Count duMas, I request an audience with the king."

Naturally it took the men a while to accept that a cat could speak. They also felt obliged to search him and his sack for weapons before taking him to the royal banquet hall where the king, his daughter, and a handful of courtiers and ladies were enjoying hot beverages. The scents of cocoa and coffee made Hunter's nose itch, but he kept from sneezing. Instead, he drew up to his full height and bowed.

"My master, the Count duMas from the next kingdom over, sends you a little gift and offers his advice on the matter of war you're facing."

"A talking cat!" Everyone started speaking at once, and Hunter had to wait in his bowed stance for quite a while before the king managed to call everyone to reason. From the corners of his eyes he noticed the calculating look of Felicitas, as if she was trying to remember where she'd seen him before. He hoped his disguise would be good enough.

"Stand straight, dear Mr. Cat." The king was a portly man dressed in dark velvet. His eyes took in his visitor and he scratched his beard. "So, your master … what would he want for his help? And what kind of help could we expect?"

"I am but a messenger with a little gift." The cat bowed again. "My master would be most pleased to discuss these matters in his castle if you'd care for a visit."

"I don't know your master." The king waved and a servant came, took the sack, and looked in.

"Partridges, sir. I will take them directly to the kitchen" He took the sack away.

The king's eyes lit up. "I'm especially fond of partridges."

"That is no secret for my master, your Majesty." Hunter bowed once more. "He sees a lot of he's so inclined."

"In that case he's either a mechanic or a sorcerer." The king pulled his lips into a smile but his gaze remained wary. "I will think about your master's offer, Mr. Cat. You do understand that I cannot accept his invitation without learning a little more about him."

"That is perfectly reasonable, your Majesty. Would you allow him to ask for a little boon meanwhile?"

The king's brow wrinkled but he held his smile which Hunter took to be a sign to continue.

"I am sure you've got plenty of miniature paintings of your beautiful daughter. If you'd send one along, my master's gratitude couldn't be greater since he lost his heart to her."

"He doesn't even know me," Princess Felicitas chimed in. "And I don't know him. Sending a picture might indicate an interest that isn't intended."

"Rest assured that he is well aware of those facts. He'd never dare to voice any wishes without mutual understanding." Hunter licked his lips to suppress a grin. If only the princess knew. After some more arguing, a servant handed him a miniature of the princess wrapped in a white lace handkerchief. Bowing, he took his leave.

🐾 🐾 🐾

Alexander suppressed a jawn. Sitting in the sun in the clearing with the unicorn's pond wasn't his idea of fun. The hare roasting over a fire he had built was already well done. Where was that cat? He'd said it wouldn't take long. Much longer and their food would get burnt. Alexander got up and began to pace until he heard something. Hadn't that been a rustling in the shrubs at the rim of the clearing?

"Hunter?"

The cat walked out of the bushes tail held high not wearing his clothes but dragging a bundle along. "Here I am, master. I brought you a little gift."

Curious, Alexander examined the bundle. Aside from Hunter's clothes he found a pair of underpants of a fabric so fine that it snatched at his coarse skin.

"That's silk," Hunter explained. "All the highborn wear it. Get used to it."

Since Alexander had already learned that protesting Hunters orders didn't change a thing, he set the white, most likely stolen pants aside and took out the last item. His breath caught. Felicitas! The picture showed her semblance with utmost accuracy which made his heartbeat speed up.

"Did she give it to you?"

"A servant did. A princess can't be seen touching a talking cat." Hunter cocked his head. "I think I'll repeat this visit a couple of times."

"Did she know it was for me?" Alexander's gaze bored into the cat's. Would he tell the truth? Would the magical bond force him to? What did being his master mean anyway? One thing was sure. Hunter wouldn't tell him.

"I told her it was for her suitor." Hunter grinned and pointed to the hare roasting over the fire. "Let's eat. I'm hungry."

Alexander kissed the picture and put it into the pocket of his jacket before he shared the hare with Hunter. The cat watched his every move which made Alexander itchy.

"What's wrong? Do I have two heads?"

"It's your table manners." Hunter hooked a claw into a piece of meat he'd cut from the hare's shoulder, lifted it to his mouth, and nibbled. "If you want to marry a princess, you've got a lot to learn."

"I'm so sorry," Alexander's voice dripped with sarcasm. "Why don't I get cutlery? And while I'm at it, a house and a title too. Oh, I remember. I spent the last of my money on your clothes."

"Don't worry about the house and the title. They'll be yours in due time. But table manners is something I can't give you. You'll have to learn them if you want to impress a princess."

"I knew I'd seen you again, Mr. Cat." The bushes at the rim of the clearing rustled again, and the princess stepped out. "And he's right about table manners, you know?"

Alexanders throat went so dry that he found it hard to swallow the meat he'd just put in his mouth. The princess had heard them. Now she knew that he was a vagabond. Surely she no longer wanted to associate with him. Aside from broad shoulders he had nothing to offer.

"It's your lucky day though." Felicitas smiled. "Along with the picnic I brought a plate and knife, spoon, and fork. I can teach you how to do it right."

"What a good idea." Hunter stretched. "When you'll meet the king you'll at least be prepared. I'll go and hunt some more partridges." He slipped away.

Alexander cleared his throat but still found it difficult to speak. "Why did you come?"

"Well, I thought this Count duMas and his talking cat a little strange." Felicitas took the dish from a bundle she was carrying. "Also, I was quite sure I'd seen that cat before. With you. So I put two and two together."

"Are you angry?"

"Because you're trying to impress my father?" She smiled. "How could I. I still don't see how your cat will get him to agree to a marriage, but the war prince most definitely is no alternative we can agree to."

She didn't love him. Alexander's heart felt as if Hunter had dug his claws in. She only considered him the lesser of two evils. He tried hard not to let his sorrow show. "I will not ask for your hand if it displeases you so."

Felicitas eyebrows went up and she studied him for a moment. Then, her pearly laughter rang through the clearing. "I'm an idiot. I used courtier-talk, and you completely misunderstood. Sorry." She put her hand on his arm, and fire sped through his body. He gasped.

"What I meant was, that I like you a lot," she said. "Probably I'm even in love with you, I don't know yet. After all, I've never been in love before. But I like you enough that the idea of getting married to you is enticing. Remember that I've know all my life that I wouldn't be allowed to marry for love. And I'm not sure how love fee…"

Alexander bent forward and closed her mouth with a kiss mid-word. His heart hammered in his chest like one of the newfangled steam engines. She tasted of strawberries and sugar, and after a second of hesitation, she returned his kiss with fervor. His brain burst into color. All thought fled. Thundering blood in his ears. Strawberry fireworks in his mind. The soft, soft skin of her cheeks under his fingers. Reactions in regions of his body he didn't really want to think about.

Felicitas withdrew, and he moaned. Her eyes sparked with mirth. "Enticing, as I said. Very enticing. Now let's concentrate on proper behavior at a dinner table. After all, your cat's plan might depend on it."

Learning had never been harder, life never been more confusing. Alexander's heart didn't slow down and the roaring blood made it hard to understand the instructions, but he did his best. Every time he managed to do something to Felicitas satisfaction, another kiss sent him to heaven … and to hell at the same time. How could he ever hope to accept her hand in marriage if the king didn't even know he existed and was faced with a war hungry prince set on taking Felicitas by force if necessary?

With all his heart he longed to grab her and run away. But what could he offer her aside from his love? He knew very well that it took more than fresh air and love to live, and while he was used to stale bread and plain water, surely Felicitas would soon get fed up. Still, he savored every kiss he got. When his table manners had improved enough for the day, Felicitas put her arms around him and hugged him.

"I'm so proud of you." She lifted her face to his and allowed him to press his lips against hers once more. Alexander closed his arms around her, digging his fingers into the mane of her hair, trying to feel her with every fiber of his being. Oh, how he longed to keep her like this forever and a day.

"Isn't that a little premature?" Hunter asked, and the glee in his voice was unmistakable.

Felicitas and Alexander ripped apart and blushed simultaneously. But they didn't need to say anything because Hunter already went on. "Can you stitch, princess?"

The next few days developed a rhythm that Alexander liked a lot. He slept well since the princess had provided him with a warm blanket for the nights. In the mornings, Hunter would take a load of partridges to the king, returning around noon with the princess not far behind. When he left to catch the next day's supply, Alexander improved his skills in everything he'd need to appear the Count Hunter named him to be, spurned by Felicitas kisses, while she stitched a coat of arms with white thread into the silken underpants the cat had brought.

"I don't understand what use the coat of arms will be. No one will ever see it," Felicitas said for the umpteenth time. "I just wish Hunter would let us know more about his plan. Under the right circumstances, father would accept you as a Count at face value, but at some point he'll be looking into your background and that'll be the end of this charade."

Alexander shared her worry, but trusted Hunters plan. He'd already gotten so much more than he'd ever dared to dream of. He was ready to enjoy the time being and life on the memories for the rest of his life. "What I'm wondering is why Hunter's so dead set on us getting married. I mean even if he can talk he's only a cat. Why would the happiness of to people concern him?"

"None of your business." As always, Hunter's appearance made Alexander flinch. The cat could be incredibly silent. Hunter spit out some feathers. "I just hope I won't have to catch partridges until doomsday."

"If you'd let us know what you're waiting for, we could be much more helpful," Felicitas pointed out. "I mean, with me you've got a spy at Court. I can recount how much my father enjoys the birds you provide him with. His mood has improved so much that he's planning an outing for tomorrow. He's heard of a witch close to the border of his kingdom, and thinks that as a citizen of his realm, she could be convinced to help him. He would dearly love to decline the war prince's offer."

"Finally!" Hunter stretched. To Alexander it looked as if he was growing. "OK, princess. Time for you to go. Make your father take you along tomorrow and bring the warmest coat you've got in your wardrobe."

"But the weather is fine." Felicitas frowned. Her gaze wandered to Alexander. "And I don't want to go yet."

"Can't be helped." Hunter stretched and hung the sack with his prey on a branch to keep smaller animals from reaching it. "You need to be there tomorrow. With your coat."

Hunter had never anticipated how hard it was to separate two people in love. In the end, Felicitas only left because he told her that he intended to introduce Alexander to his father-in-law to-be the next day. When she had left, his master had built up another fire and fried the mushrooms Hunter had brought him on a pan the princess had given him. Silently, he shared the food equally even though it was barely enough for one. Only when Alexander had cleaned the dishes and watched the fire die down to embers did he talk again.

"Hunter?" He didn't look up, so the cat acknowledged him with a grunt. "I just wanted to thank you."

"What for?" Once more Hunter was taken by surprise.

"For trying. These have been the most wonderful days of my life. I know that whatever trick you've got up your sleeve might backfire, but I don't care." Alexander wrapped himself into his blanket. "Whatever the king will do, whether I end up dangling from a rope or forced from the kingdom, I wanted you to know that I truly appreciate what you're trying to achieve. You're my best friend."

"Nonsense." Hunter cleared his throat. Why did he feel like he'd swallowed a frog? "The king will take you in with open arms."

"If you say so." Alexander smiled at him, and all of a sudden, Hunter felt warm from the inside out. Unblinking, he watched the human curl up beside the dying fire. Friend … The word echoed through his mind. He'd never had a friend. Was the strange fuzzy feeling part of the deal? Would it stop if Alexander found out that he intended him to play the role of the goat meant to lure the tiger?

He knew that with the king, the princess and his master approaching the witch's castle, she'd be preoccupied. And since she didn't know he had regained his ability to use magic and gathered enough power for a hard and fast attack, he was fairly certain that he could kill her and thus win his freedom. But that meant leaving the humans to fend for themselves, and without magic that was a suicide mission.

Hunter cringed. Life had been so much easier when it was still black and white, bad humans and good magical creatures. He wasn't anything remotely reminiscent of a human. He should be free of the shackles of friendship or love. So why did he suddenly feel responsible for Alexander's happiness? Was there a way he could pull off his plan without endangering his master?

He spent the rest of the night trying to analyze his feelings and looking for ways to adapt his plan, but there was nothing he could see that might work.

When Alexander woke in the early morning, Hunter felt as if he'd been run over by one of the new steam cars some humans were so fond of. He shook himself. He couldn't afford to let his decisions be ruled by empathy. Maybe he'd find a way to adapt his plans as they were unfolding. Until then he'd have to do what needed to be done.

"Let's go, and do pack the silken underpants," he said as soon as Alexander had finished eating his last bit of bread. The young man obeyed. Wordlessly he picked up the sack with the clothes.

Hunter took the lead. Since the king intended to visit the witch, he knew exactly where he needed to go. After all, he'd haunted the area around the castle long enough that the witch had appropriated after she'd made him the miller's slave.

So he took Alexander to a small valley in the foothills of the witch's property where the king had to pass through. A small lake huddled between the gently rolling hills with a brook coming from the mountains rising behind. It was surrounded brushes and trees standing in groups in the otherwise grassy hills. The view from a rocky outcrop further down the valley would be perfect to notice the royal coach long before it got this far.

"Undress," he ordered and watched Alexander take off his clothes. A golden sparkle caught his attention. He pointed to his master's chest. "What's that?"

"It's a brass medallion. Mother said, I had been wearing it under my clothes when she got me." Alexander covered it with his hand. "I'm not going to take it off."

"There's absolutely no need to." Hunter could have screamed for joy, although how he had missed the medallion before was beyond him. "By the way, it's gold, not brass. Now take the underwear off, too."

"But …"

"No buts. You'll wear the silk pants I gave you." Hunter slipped into his own disguise and pointed to the sack. "I'll hide the sack with your clothes and blanket so the king won't see it. As soon as I call, jump into the water. It shouldn't be a long wait."

"Why?" Shivering Alexander stared him down. "You never tell me anything but expect me to jump into a lake I've never even tried. There could be a monster in it."

"There isn't. I checked." Hunter told the truth. He'd double checked every possible path the king could take, and this was the best place for the kind of ambush he had in mind. "The water is just a little cold. And you won't need to stay in for long."

"If I catch a cold, you're to blame." Alexander rubbed his arms with his hands but walked as close to the water as he could without getting wet yet. Hunter grabbed the sack with the clothes, hid them deep between a couple of prickly bushes and sat on the rocky outcrop. In silence they waited for the king. It took much longer than Hunter had anticipated. Luckily the sun was still warm and thus the morning chill soon dissipated. Hunter noticed Alexander relax and sit. They had to wait nearly until lunch time before a cloud of dust announced the king's coming. Soon it revealed a spec of white. When the box-shape of the coach and the four horses were clearly visible, Hunter called, "They'll be here in five minutes."

Alexander walked into the water without hesitation. "Woa! Is that cold." He stood in the lake with the water reaching up to his belly button hugging himself with muscular arms. Water dripped off his shoulders, and the medallion sparkled in the sun. "It's even colder than the water in the unicorn's pond. I'm not ducking again."

"What did you expect." Hunter grinned. "The water comes from the glaciers in the mountains."

"How long do I have to stay in here?"

"Only a little while." Hunter gazed at his master, admiring his handywork. The young man's body, muscular and slender through the hard work he the miller had forced him to do, reacted just like he had expected. Due to the cold, the blood concentrated on keeping the inner organs warm. Thus the skin lost most of its suntanned look.

Hunter turned back to the road. The coach was now near enough that the travelers inside could hear him, so he jumped off the rocky outcrop and began to call for help, waving his hat.

The coach stopped right in front of him, and the king looked out of the window. "My dear Mr. Cat. What happened?"

"On his annual voyage to inspect the borders of his property, my master decided to go swimming. By the time I arrived, someone had stolen his horse and weapons, even his clothes without him noticing. Thank the gods for your arrival." The cat bowed deeply. "If you'd be so kind to lend us a coat or a blanket. The water is icy since it comes from the mountain glaciers."

"He can have my coat," Princess Felicitas said. "The weather has improved so much that I don't need it any more."

"Too kind of you, your highness." Hunter bowed again to hide his smile. "The coat of a woman as beautiful as you will be a delight to wear for Count duMas."

The king waved wordlessly. Immediately two servants jumped off of the back of the coach, took the coat Felicitas handed them and hurried ahead to the lake. The coach followed more slowly, giving the 'Count' time to get out of the water and into the midnight blue flowing robe. When they arrived, both the king and the princess left the coach. Hunter introduced Alexander with his new name, and the princess invited him to travel with them. Upon a nudge from Hunter, Alexander agreed and followed her into the coach.

Before entering too, the king said to Hunter, "I thought these lands belong to a witch."

"That is a misconception." Hunter grinned, fully aware that he was showing his incisors. "She used to live here, but my master' defeated her. She didn't stand a chance."

"Oh!" The king's eyebrows rose and his forehead wrinkled. Hunter could practically see where his thoughts were headed.

"Why don't you come and visit my master's castle? He'll be delighted to have you and your daughter. He doesn't get many visitors."

"That'd be wonderful." The king's face lit up. After all he didn't know he was being sent into a trap as the bait. That was one problem down and only two more to go – the witch and her apprentice.

"I will run ahead and tell the castle staff of your arrival."

"It is a pity to see such an interesting and intelligent creature go, but I understand the need." The king nodded and climbed aboard.

"Do enjoy the trip, and take your time. The servants will appreciate any additional minute they can get," Hunter said. Then, he turned and ran off, his cape streaming behind him like a flag.

🐾 🐾 🐾

After polite introductions, the king smiled at Alexander and said, "So, you defeated the Witch from the Mountains?"

Alexander's throat went dry immediately. He coughed. "Well, I …"

"Not so shy, dear Count, Mr. Cat told me everything already."

"Oh, ehm, well, in that case …" Alexander's thoughts raced. How could Hunter claim something like that? To defeat a witch one needed magic, and he didn't have a single drop of it in his blood.

"See, I've got this idea and was wondering if it would be of interest to you." The king slipped forward a little, put one hand on Alexander's knee, and pointed at Felicitas with the other. "This is my beautiful daughter. She could be yours if you'd agree to protect my kingdom from the war prince."

"The war prince?" The king's words did what the icy water hadn't managed, they chilled him to the marrow.

"Father!" Felicitas voice cut through Alexander's confusion and fear.

"I told you before that I'm the one to decide whom you will marry, Felicitas." The king frowned. "I've been trying to find a way to avoid giving you to the war prince, and it seems that the Count is our only chance."

"I do not object, dear father. If you think a marriage with Count duMas is the solution to your problem, I will comply." A smile lit up her whole face. "However, the Count has had a harrowing experience. Don't you think we should give him some time to recover? Why don't we wait until after lunch to talk business? Let us enjoy the voyage instead."

"Splendid idea, my dear." The king leaned back into his seat. "I just hope we'll have partridges for lunch."

The princess turned to Alexander and winked with one eye. "I am sure Mr. Cat will find the perfect solution for all our problems."

Her smile made Alexander's heart melt and harden at the same time. For her he'd be the greatest sorcerer in the world. He just hoped the cat's plans didn't involve the need to prove his magical skills. But right now, Felicitas words had calmed his panic enough that he could enjoy the scenery behind the windows and the king's friendly small talk.

Hunter raced up the hill. The trees that grew in smaller or bigger patches all over the foothills, grew more numerous the closer he got to the cliff with the castle.

Crash!

He stopped in his tracks. Had the witch noticed him or the coach already?

"Be careful! Ya nearly killed ma." The voice came from a small cluster of firs close to the road the coach had to take to master the steep incline.

"Pushin' trees is harder dan it looks," a second voice answered. "Never meant ta hit ya. But dese stuppid trees always topple da wrong direction.'"

On tiptoes, Hunter walked closer. Two trolls were carrying two felled trees to a pile they'd already made beside the road.

Hunter thought that the trolls would be perfect to counter the war prince's threat. He'd be loath to attack trolls. They weren't known for intelligence but they sure as hell could fight. Hunter's mind reeled with the ramifications of his idea. He could probably even use it against the witch which meant Alexander didn't necessarily need to be his pawn sacrifice. It was truly brilliant.

"What does da witch needs dese for anyway?" The younger troll frowned, showing how hard he was thinking.

"Da new miller wants dem. Dunno what for dough." The second one dropped his tree and turned to fetch another one when Hunter stepped from the bushes.

"Good evening, my dear fellows."

"Food!" The younger troll grabbed for Hunter, but a magical slap stopped his hand mid-air. He winced, he sucked on his fingers.

The older was more cautious. "What da ya want?"

"Am I assuming right that you're servants of the witch?" He didn't really need to ask. He could sense the tendrils of black magic she'd wrapped around the pair. They resembled his own ties.

The frown on the foreheads of the trolls grew deeper, their gaze darkened.

"Witch evil!"

"I do agree, but I have a plan." Hunter tried to look as confident as he should feel. "Wouldn't you like to be free to return to your beloved mountains?"

"You got plan?" The older troll asked.

"Me not fight," the younger announced. "Witch fight unfair. Does hurt bad."

"Oh, you don't need to fight. You only need to pledge loyalty to my master, the Count duMas." Hunter loosened several of the tendrils of black magic surrounding the trolls and wove them in with his own. He felt the draining of his magic increase, but for once he rejoiced. If all went well, this would be the witch's downfall. "When the witch is dead, my master will release you. I promise by the honor of the Rolling Stone."

The trolls looked at each other, their constantly changing facial expressions showed how hard they were thinking. After a while they nodded. Hunter was pleased; sometimes it paid off to understand magical creatures as well as he did.

"We swear fealty to da Count duMa," they said in unison.

"Da guy seems nicer dan the witch. Can we stop pushing trees den?" the younger wanted to know.

"For now," Hunter said. "But as soon as you see a white coach come up that way, pick up the biggest trees you've got and salute to the Count with them."

"Can do." The older troll slumped and sat while the younger dug around in a bundle on his hip, handing him something to eat that Hunter didn't want to look at too closely. He diverted the last few strands of the witch's magic and off he went again.

A little further up the path he neared a couple of stony fields close to a village. Several goblins led oxen with ploughs over them, turning the soil like farmers. Hunter noticed the magic threads surrounding them even before he opened his mouth to speak.

"Hark my words. Swear fealty to the Count duMas and you shall get your true form back." This promise was easy to keep. They already began changing back into humans while he moved their magic threads over to his already bulging bundle.

"We swear!" They shouted together. When they noticed the changes due to getting pulled out of their spells, they rejoiced and praised the cat. It was more difficult to get away from them than it had been with the trolls. In some respect the slow thinkers were easier to handle. But Hunter managed and soon he was on his way again.

The last bunch of people he encountered were some mer-people standing in the shallow river fishing. Their arms and torsos looked blue with the cold, but the baskets on the bank were only half full. *What a nasty way to exploit humans,* Hunter thought. He blushed under his fur when he realized that his previous idea of killing of all humans to avenge his capture was even worse. Again he suggested the same bargain he'd offered the troll and the goblins and took on their magical burden. Somehow the relief on their faces when their bodies began to change back to their human form because he collected their spells tugged on his heartstrings. Best not to linger. Emotions could be dangerous for the likes of him. He hurried onward up the hill until he saw the white walls of the castle rising out of the rock. *It looks like a white flower on a cliff,* he mused, *and houses the darkest danger I ever encountered.*

It was time now to decide whether he should proceed with his original plan or think of a new, equally efficient one. *Well, Alexander and the king will need a while longer. I think I'll use the time to find out more about the witch. Maybe I can discover a weakness I wasn't aware of before.* With a sigh he took off his coat, hat, and boots, hid them, and slipped between the cracks of the rocks carrying the castle.

"This forest is astounding, dear Count," the king said. "Where do you sell the trees you harvest?"

"Ah well, you know ..." Alexander didn't know what to say. Luckily the king didn't seem to expect an answer. He kept on raving about the scenery they were passing through.

"Your cat didn't promise too much," he said. "If one disregards the sorry state of the roads, this country is extremely beautiful."

"Speaking of my cat," Alexander said, glad to be able to change the subject. "Did he tell you where he went?"

"He meant to alert your castle's staff to our coming." Felicitas smiled at him, but Alexander only felt dread descend on him. A castle? Where did Hunter intend to find one and how would he convince its inhabitants that it belonged to Count duMas? Oblivious to Felicitas beauty, Alexander worried more with every meter they drove.

Suddenly the coach lurched to a halt.

"Hail da Count daMas!" Two voices boomed loud enough that every bird in a mile took flight. The horses whinnied and rose although the coachman managed to keep them from running, and the king went pale.

Fighting to keep control over his bladder, Alexander stepped out of the coach. The trolls had hailed him, and even if he didn't see what he could do to save Felicitas and her father, he would do his best.

"Ehm…" He cleared his throat. "I am Count duMas." It felt strange to use a name that wasn't his, but it seemed to be his only protection. When the two trolls knelt on the ground, their trees still resting on their shoulders, he wondered what Hunter had told them.

"Look." The bigger one pointed to a pile of trees beside the road. "We did a lotta harvestin. Like it?"

Alexander nodded. An idea sneaked into his numbed brain. "Why don't you take the rest of the day off?" When he noticed the frown on the trolls' faces, he added, "We're celebrating the king's visit to my realm."

"Da Count is too friendly." One of the trolls bowed, nudging the other until he followed his example. Then, they got to their feet, laid their trees onto the pile beside the road and ambled away down the hill.

Alexander sighed with relief. In the coach, he heard the king do the same.

"Impressive," the king said. "How did you convince them to work for you."

"Well …" Again he didn't know what to say, so he climbed back into the carriage thinking frantically for a plausible explanation.

Felicitas helped him out. "I'm presuming Mr. Cat hired them. After all, trolls are quite common in this part of the country. And they do make great timber men, don't you think?"

"Oh yes. It's so hard to find good personell these days," the king said. When the coach went on and bumped through pothole after pothole, he added, "Maybe you should hire some more to improve the condition of your roads."

"We never expected much traffic." Alexander tried not to sound apologetic without success.

"Ah, but my daughter and I are planning on an increased frequency of our visits, now that we found we've got such a charming neighbor." The king smiled. Suddenly Alexander realized that Felicitas father wouldn't mind at all if he asked *the* question. Of course he didn't. After all he didn't know what Hunter was up to and whether he would be Count duMas for much longer. He didn't want to gain Felicitas hand by deceiving his father-in-law to-be.

"Don't you think it'd be a good idea to get to know each other better?" Felicitas asked. Her warm hand with the slender fingers slipped into his and squeezed. He smiled at her and decided to ask the king for her hand if Hunter managed to make the title of Count permanent.

"It surely is tempting. I might be able to sell some of the timber to carpenters in your kingdom," he said, pretending to be the Count Hunter had named him to be. As they went on, he and the king developed ideas on how to better connect the Count's country with the kingdom.

🐾 🐾 🐾

Unseen Hunter reached a balcony above the main hall, normally used by musicians, although many servants hurried to and fro. The poor people were invisible except for their hands. Maybe the witch didn't like their looks. He also discovered plenty that stood rooted to the spot, without breathing, still like statues. Yet more tendrils of black magic joined the bundle he carried. The weight pressed him closer and closer to the ground. Still he smiled. It felt good to deprive the witch from the system she'd set up to gather magic from every corner of her lands. The best part was that she wouldn't notice until she needed a lot of magic at once – such was the drawback of black magic. A white witch would have sensed the changing of the natural structure of her spells.

Hunter peered through a gap in the wooden balustrade at the scene below. The witch had assumed the shape of a portly man who looked just like the man in the picture above the mantle.

"To me, old friend." She saluted the picture with a pitcher of wine.

"Why do you keep doing that?" The miller's second son pushed away his food laden plate and got up from the table. "You dumped his brat in the gorge after Pa killed him ages ago."

"Your father deprived me from torturing the only man I always wanted." The witch shot round. "I just wish my brother had died without making that new will. Then I could have had his soul to remind him what he still owes me."

"So do I. I hate having to protect my brother." Oliver picked up his own wine, walked over to her, and clinked his pitcher against hers. "To new beginnings."

A waft of warm air drifted up from the hall below and carried with it the bitter-sweet scent of yew tree poison in the witch's wine. At the same time Hunter noticed yet another black magic tendril. It was draining Oliver, and it was a lot bigger than all the other tendrils he'd gathered together. He had to get close enough to steal that tendril too.

"To your health," the witch said and emptied her pitcher in one gulp. Hunter felt Oliver's anticipation, but nothing happened. The witch returned to her meal as if nothing had happened. When Oliver turned to walk to his place, Hunter could see the disappointment on his face and grinned. How could the youngster believe that a black witch hadn't prepared against all the poisons in her possession?

"I'll go to the lab and try the shape shifter spell again," Oliver said. Without waiting for the witch's answer, he left the hall.

Hunter hurried downstairs. He had been in this castle long before the witch arrived, so he knew very well in which room she had set up the laboratory. He dashed to the place where he had left his clothes, grabbed the bundle, and hurried back, reaching the door to the lab mere minutes before Oliver. Hurriedly, he slipped into his finery and walked toward the footsteps. When he turned a corner, he nearly bumped into the witch's apprentice – just like he had planned.

"Stop it right there, fiend." The miller's younger son pointed a stick with a glowing tip at him. His eyes narrowed, and Hunter imagined how his thoughts raced. "You ... you are my father's cat. Why are you ... Oh, I see! But you won't find a way to break your spell, not even if you burgle my aunt's lab."

"I did not come to burgle, I came to plead." Hunter was busy taking the gigantic thread of black magic from Oliver and tying it to his bundle. Speaking became harder. "Surely the witch is open to a bargain."

This new train of thought obviously kept Oliver from thinking about how the cat had come in. He motioned with his magic wand. "Take the lead, and don't even think about trying to escape. I know who you are and how to handle you. It was one of the first spells aunt taught me."

Hunter was fairly sure that Oliver wouldn't be able to confront him properly. He'd memorized too many of the witch's short cut spells to weave a true spell, but he didn't take any chances. Gingerly she stepped past the young man and walked up the stairs. It was hard work since the huge bulk of black magic rested on him like a big boulder. Still, he made it to the hall where the witch in her male disguise was still eating.

"Look who I found sneaking around the castle," Oliver said to her.

She just yawned, got up, walked around the cat, and said, "There's nothing he can do. He's too well tied up in my spell." With a frown she bent forward and sniffed the air as if trying to gauge the intensity of the spell via scent. "Strange. I never thought it would be this strong. Well, that way it's even harder to break."

Despite his loathing, Hunter was fascinated. He had known that different witches sensed magic in different ways, but never experienced it first hand. Would she notice when he began part two of his new plan?

"Where's that idiot boy, your master?" The witch kicked him lightly against the shin, and pain shot up Hunter's leg.

"I left him half naked in the foothills." Hunter was proud that he didn't need to lie. A black witch always noticed lies. Luckily she couldn't determine whether he told her everything or just part of the truth.

"Why have you come?" The witch cocked her head and frowned which made her fake pudgy face contort as if in pain. Hunter longed to set his new plan into motion, but the witch was still too focused on him.

"My master wants to marry a princess." Again, this was the whole truth. Hunter knew he was walking a very thin line. "As you're well aware, he needs to be of noble blood to do so."

"Does he really think he can find a king to knight him?" The witch laughed, but her calculating gaze never left him. "I just wonder why you didn't stick with him. After all, it should be in your interest to marry him off to a princess."

"Oh, he doesn't need to be knighted. He already is of noble blood. All he needs for that is a proof." Hunter looked up at the picture of the previous Count, the one the miller had murdered and the witch was now impersonating. It suited him fine that he had recognized Alexander's medallion. That way he could stick to the truth.

The witch caught his gaze, came to exactly the conclusion Hunter had wanted her to have, and paled. "But I threw the infant into the river's ravine."

"His mother's love and her blessing spell protected him. It wasn't hard for me to pull him out further downstream." Back when he had rescued the Count's son without knowing his identity, Hunter hadn't been able to explain why he felt compelled to do so. He'd just been glad that it had secured him the love and gratitude of the miller's wife. Now he congratulated himself. "Hiding him directly under your nose pleased me no end."

The witch's boot connected hard with his ribs. With a yowl, Hunter flew through the air. The tendrils around him made it hard to twist in the way he usually could, so he landed on his side with a hard thud. He moaned and pretended to be unconscious. The witch ignored him, already issuing orders.

"Guards, man the ramparts." Invisible people ran out of the room, their hands, the only visible parts, closed tightly around spears and halberds.

"Oliver, you'll jump to the foothill. If you see the boy there, kill him. If not, come back immediately."

"Must I?" The miller's son frowned. "He's only a stupid idiot. He won't be able to cause much trouble."

"He is the son of one of the most talented white witches I ever encountered. I only got the better of her because she was grieving for her husband." The witch in the body of the Count clenched her hands to fists. "Even if he doesn't have a drop of talent for magic in his blood, her blessing spell might still be active, and that has the potential to destroy both of us. Off you go. I need to prepare for battle in case he shows up here."

Just as planned by Hunter, Oliver vanished. The cat had to force himself not to purr. Carefully he undid one thread of black magic after the other and tied them to the witch. She was so busy flipping through a big, black book that she didn't notice. When Hunter fixed the last of the borrowed threads to her – unfortunately he couldn't undo his own bonds – her body flickered. She abandoned the likeness of Alexander's father and returned to her own form. Mumbling spells she still didn't notice. Hunter breathed deeply. The time had come. Soon he'd either be free … or dead.

By the time the coach had left the fishermen, Alexander was ready to believe that he really was the Count duMas. The oldest fisherman had insisted that he looked just like the previous Count 'just younger and slimmer', as he had put it.

"Methinks you've got a rich country, dear Count." The king patted his arm. "Splendid, splendid."

"Please do call me Alexander, your Majesty." Alexander's heart contracted at the suggestion, but Felicitas smile told him he'd done the right thing.

"I'm delighted to comply." The king looked from his daughter to Alexander and back. "Especially since it seems my daughter has taken a liking to you."

Alexander's cheeks grew hot.

"She's not alone in that regard." The king leaned back and crossed his legs, smiling. "Lend me a couple of your trolls against the war prince, and I'll give you her hand in marriage."

Before Alexander could answer anything, the coach lurched to another stop. The door crashed open and Oliver reached in. His fingers closed around the coat the princess had given Alexander, and he pulled him out of the coach, throwing him to the ground with a fluid motion.

"Freeze!" Oliver pointed his magic wand to the coach, and the king, the princess, the coachman and the servants stopped moving. With a snarl on his face he turned to Alexander. "How dare you come here?"

"Unfreeze them right now or …" The built up anger of the last few years combined with the worry about Felicitas and her father propelled Alexander to his feet. He lunged at his step-brother. His fist slammed into Oliver's nose.

Caught by surprise, the witch's apprentice stumbled backwards. Blood ran from his nose. Alexander attacked again, but this time Oliver vanished before his fist connected with his chest. He reappeared a few steps to the side. With a scream of rage he pointed his wand at Alexander and yelled a word, sharp like a knife and colder than ice. It sliced into Alexander's chest, numbing him to the core. Doubling over, he felt the spell drain his life from him, but before he could pass out, a lullaby drifted to the surface of his consciousness. Unsure whether he was dreaming, or if he was seeing by an angel, Alexander stared at the woman who cradled his head humming a song he'd known all his life. He remembered her face. He had known it from the first day of his life.

"Mother?" he whispered, and she nodded and smiled. Her love cocooned him like a warm embrace. She helped him to his feet. The air around them shone brightly, making it hard to see anything around him. Still Alexander could make out the black tendrils floating from Oliver's wand toward him. The light swallowed them effortlessly, and soon the miller's son toppled over and fell to the ground. The woman stroked Alexander's hair and blew him a kiss before she vanished and took the light with her.

Alexander stared after her, until soft lips touched his. Only then did his gaze focus on the beauty in his arms. Felicitas had left the coach and was standing on tiptoes in front of him. Her hands held his face, and her kiss sent tingles down his spine. When she noticed he had returned to reality, she let go.

"Dear me, that was quite the scare." The king grabbed his arm. "We already thought the sorcerer drove your mind from your body. Why didn't you tell us that you're a magician?"

"I'm not." Alexander's mind was in turmoil. What had just happened? He gazed at Oliver who was lying on the ground like a crumpled piece of paper. His step-brother was still breathing, but Alexander knew with a strange certainty that he'd never do magic again, although he couldn't say how he knew that. *I think I'll have to ask Hunter,* he thought.

"Are you alright?" Felicitas wide eyes were filled with worry.

"Yes, I am." He kissed her reassuringly. "Let's go. The castle isn't far, and somehow I have the feeling that Hunter could do with a little help."

Painfully aware of the strands of magic of his curse, Hunter slipped out of his hat and boots and stood up on four legs. He threw his coat off of his shoulders and unsheathed his claws. It felt good to be hunting again. For starters, he pretended he was trying to flee.

The witch shot around, pointed her index finger at him, and said a word. A flash shot toward him and caught him in the chest. Using whatever little magic he could gather, Hunter pushed it into the tendrils that connected his magic with the witch's.

"Autch." She frowned and studied him closer but didn't seem to notice anything was amiss. "So you finally discovered a loophole to magic. Well, that won't help you."

In the blink of an eye, she turned herself into a lion and jumped forward. Hunter needed all his agility to avoid her jaws.

"I'll get you." Mid-jump the lion turned into a wolf and snapped at Hunter's tail. Hunter jumped to the chandelier with a yowl, and the wolf turned into a raven. Hunter fled again, and the witch adapted her body. But true bodily changes cost a lot of energy. The witch grew weaker, and that was what Hunter had hoped for. With every change she made, her own store of magic diminished. Knowing she'd soon be forced to collect more magic, Hunter did his best to avoid her snapping jaws or beaks or fangs. Like any other cat he kept screaming, partially because it felt good and partially because it distracted the witch.

Swaying slightly she turned from a hyena into an eagle. Talons first, she attacked again and nailed Hunter's tail to the floor. He screamed in frustration.

How much longer until his plan worked? Frantically, he pawed the big bird, wondering why the witch didn't use the beak to hurt him.

"Well, that was a nice chase." She panted. "Lot's of fun. But now I need to take acre of the real threat. No, what shall I do with you?" She cocked the eagle's head and blinked a couple of times. "I know, I'll squeeze you to death."

Hunter could feel her gathering her magic for the spell, but there wasn't much left. She used a few words that sucked magic through the threads of her spells and initiated the change. For a moment, the outline of an elephant hovered in the place of the eagle, but it vanished after but a heartbeat, and the witch was returned momentarily to her true body. Hunter grinned when the began to shrink, even though his curse was sucking away his magic. Loosing magic so rapidly felt as if someone was trying to skin his cat form alive, and he screamed with pain. However, he didn't stop grinning. His plan worked.

"What the ..." For a split second, the miniature witch's beautiful face filled with fear, then it began to change. Hair sprouted everywhere, her nose elongated, and her ears grew. "What did you do to my magic?"

Hunter didn't answer although he would have liked to tell her all about interferences. It hurt too much to do anything but breathe and watch the witch shrink more and more. As he had hoped, trying to pull magic through the black magic threads caused a feedback loop. And although it hurt him too, the results were all he'd hoped for and more. Since the witch had used a spell to truly change her body, what little magic she could get from Hunter's curse did it's best to give her the animal's body she had requested. A few minutes after she'd said the spell, a mouse-sized elephant ran away from Hunter. He did his best to ignore his pain and jumped.

One jump.

One bite.

One squeal.

Yuck. That tastes like excrement mixed with onions, garlic and vomit. Hunter had to force himself to swallow. But then, it was over. He felt the spells dissipate that the witch had used to pull magic from her victims including the threads connecting his curse to the witch. Very slowly his pain eased. He laid down and breathed to regain his strength. He could still feel the curse keeping him from his freedom and from most of his magic, but the dark presence of the witch was gone.

Alexander! Struggling with his weakness, he got up and walked to where he had left his clothes. A young servant girl, maybe twenty five years old, peeked through a doorway. She was fully visible from her pale blond hair to the the tip of her dark brown shoes.

"The witch is dead." Slipping into his boots, Hunter smiled at her, and she flinched but didn't leave. "We need an engagement feast for our master Count duMas."

"Count duMas is dead," the girl said. "I saw him getting murdered."

"But his son survived, and he's coming any minute." Hunter stretched and put on his hat. "Tell the others. We need to hurry."

The girl ran off, shouting at the top of her lungs. "The Count's son survived. He is coming here with his bride. Long live Count duMas!"

Something burned in Hunter's throat. He coughed. Hard.

Despite the white walls, the castle looked forbidding as the coach rolled up the last incline to the drawbridge. Studded with towers and turrets, it looked like a puzzle that hadn't been put together properly. Grim looking soldiers were standing on the ramparts, and Alexander's hands grew cold.

"I'd better get ahead and announce us," he said. "They're not really used to visitors."

"Surely they'll recognize their master." The king's eyebrows rose.

"Naturally." Alexander's thoughts raced. He needed a reason to go first. As much as he trusted Hunter, he couldn't endanger Felicitas or her father. An idea came to mind. "Unfortunately they will not be able to see me if I stay with you. And the coach is unfamiliar to them. They might overreact despite Hunter's announcement."

"Go if you think it's necessary," Felicitas said stopping another comment from her father. Relieved Alexander climbed out of the coach and walked toward the castle. From the portcullis two soldiers came running. When they reached him, one of them asked, "Are you Count duMas?"

Facing to men in chain mail with halberds, swords, and helmets, Alexander found it hard to lie, but he did his best to sound convincing. "That is my name."

After waving their halberds at the ramparts thrice, the two men knelt on the ground, accompanied by the cheering of the men above.

"Long live Count duMas," they said.

One got up and said, "Your cat alerted us to your arrival. Please come this way."

Alexander followed the man while the second one approached the coach, grabbed the horses bridles, and led them over the drawbridge. The courtyard was surprisingly wide. Maids were just putting pots with flowers everywhere, and a portly man supervised a group of youngsters rolling out a red carpet. Everyone cheered when they saw Alexander and tried to touch him somewhere. The coach stopped right at the end of the red carpet. As Alexander hurried to help Felicitas, Hunter left the castle walking over the other end of the carpet. He caught up with his master and opened the door of the coach. The king got out first.

"Dear Count, this castle is beautiful." Gazing up and around, he made room for his daughter. Felicitas took Alexander's hand and kept it. Warmth spread through him, but he was also very worried. What if anyone found out he wasn't the real Count? What if the real Count came home?

"It deems wise to find my master some decent clothes." Hunter bowed to the king. "Meanwhile the Grand Marshal will show you the castle. We will meet you in the main hall in a little while."

Reluctantly Alexander let Felicitas go and followed the cat to a bedroom the size of the mill's ground floor.

"What happened to Oliver?" Hunter asked and rummaged through a wardrobe filled with clothes that were a little too big for Alexander while listening to the tale.

He discovered an outfit that suited the young man perfectly. Alexander marveled at how soft the white, ruffled shirt felt on his skin. And the dark blue velvet of the vest went well with the black trousers. Hunter even found shoes.

"When the king has returned to his own castle tomorrow, I'll show you the treasury." Hunter wiped his whiskers with a paw. "I am sure you will make good use of its contents."

"It feels like stealing," Alexander said.

"It's previous owner won't need it any longer." Hunter shrugged. "By the way, I assumed that you'd like to ask your beloved princess an important question, so I ordered an engagement meal to be served in the main hall."

Alexander blushed, then straightened. What he was about to do would probably kill him, but he couldn't go on like this. It hurt too much.

"We need to talk about this, Hunter," he said. "I can't pretend to be Count duMas any longer. I feel like the fraud that I am. Even if it means losing Felicitas I'd rather be truthful about my origins."

"You do not know your origins, my dear." Hunter grinned, displaying his full set of teeth. "But I do. You are Count duMas."

"Impossible. How do you know?" Alexander's eyes widened and he had to sit on the bed because his knees wobbled so much. A flicker of hope made his heart beat faster. "And can you prove it?"

"Open the gold medallion you've brought. The proof is in there." Hunter pointed to the bedside table where the medallion waited to be put on again.

Gold? But ... Alexander's thoughts whirled around. Gingerly he took it and examined it more closely. For the first time he noticed a tiny bulge at the side. When he pressed it, the medallion clicked and opened. A cloud of white smoke whirled out and coalesced into the beautiful woman Alexander had already seen once. She smiled at him and blew him a kiss, forming the words "I love you, my son." Alexander understood her although no sound could be heard. When she vanished, he looked at the pictures inside. The one on the left hand showed the coat of arms Hunter had made Felicitas stitch into the silk pants, the one on the right showed his mother with a young but slightly portly man Alexander took to be his father.

"You'll find the man's portrait downstairs in the main hall," Hunter said. "Count duMas was the previous owner of this castle. The witch killed him and threw you into a deep ravine to get rid of you. But your mother's protection saved you and the rivulet down in the ravine carried you close to the mill where I pulled you out. I only realized who you where when I saw the medallion when you undressed in the foothills."

Alexander didn't listen to the end of the explanation. He put the medallion's chain around his neck and stormed from the room, down the stairs to the main hall.

Hunter couldn't help but chuckle. Humans were far more fun than he'd ever thought possible. He followed Alexander slowly and found him holding hand with Felicitas, gazing into her eyes. It was self-evident that Hunter would be free soon.

A fire cackled in the open fireplace, and delicious smells wafted over from the table. Countless servants hurried to and fro perfecting the feast. Hunter's stomach grumbled. At the same time, he spotted a hairball – the hairball he'd coughed up just a little while ago still held tiny elephant bones. With an elegant flip, he kicked it into the fire. It burst into flame immediately.

"Mr. Cat!" The king wore a smile from one ear to the other. "Isn't it marvelous? Count duMas just asked me for my daughter's hand in marriage, and I agreed. Since he's capable of commanding trolls, the war prince won't dare to attack us."

"I am sure you are right." Hunter mirrored the king's smile. "When will they marry?"

"As soon as possible. I give them my blessing."

As if on command, the young couple kissed, and Hunter felt the curse crumble and fall. Glad that he didn't have to wait for the real wedding, he stretched and twisted. His cat's body made way for his real one. So what if his face still wore a semblance? The pointy ears with the golden earring, his whiskers, his broad shoulders and slender hips in harem pants, everything was still there. Joy coursed through his veins.

"I'm free!" He shouted, grabbed Alexander and swung him around, then set him down beside Felicitas again. He kissed them both on their cheeks. "Your love set me free. Thank you. Now I can finally go home. Oh, how I have longed to be there."

"What are you?" The princess was the first to regain her voice.

"I am a djinn. The witch and the miller caught me nearly a quarter century ago when they still lived in the south. They bound me into the body of a male cat."

"You're not leaving right away, are you?" Alexander's voice trembled a little. "I'd miss you a lot, my friend."

Friend. Hunter closed his eyes. No one had ever called him a friend, not even back in the days when he lived with the other djinni. He felt his former magic seep back into him. It would take a while to recharge fully, so maybe he should stay a while longer? It might be interesting to see what a friendship might mean for him.

"I think I'll stay to the wedding." He took Alexander's and Felicitas' arms. "Shall we have lunch now? I'm starving."

BONUS STORY: WHY THE PRINCESS SLEPT ON A PEA

losely based on "The Princess and the Pea"

Jacob disengaged the gears of his lawnmower. The little steam engine puffed white clouds into the bright blue sky, and the garden surrounding him looked as if it had sprung from a fairy tale. Flowers bloomed everywhere. He sighed. This was so much better than thinking up new laws or opening a kindergarten. Fleeing his home country had been the worst and the best that ever happened to him.

The bell of the town's central hall at the foot of the castle's hill announced the lunch hour. Jacob broke a rose from one of the nearby bushes, re-engaged the lawnmower's gears without starting the cutting unit, and drove to the gardener's hut where he lived with his sister, hoping she was up already.

Ruth was still sitting in her nightdress at the kitchen table. Her pale, soft skin and her golden hair emphasized her true origin. No commoner had ever managed to keep their complexion this fair, their hands this smooth. Jacob knew that life as a gardener's sister didn't suit Ruth, but there was nothing he could do about it. He had no army at his disposal, and a twenty year old ex-prince with his seventeen year old sister weren't enough to overthrow the newly elected government of his home country. Not that he wanted to do that anyway.

"I hate this house," Ruth said when he handed her the rose. "The bed is so hard, I barely feel my body any more."

"If you found yourself a job, you'd be too tired to notice." Jacob had argued about this many times over the last three years so he didn't put much effort into his words. He knew she wouldn't budge. And he was right. As he neared the hearth, she repeated the same old phrases.

"A princess shouldn't need to work. I should be dancing with princes or stitching my wedding dress. It's all I learned." She looked at him with tears in her eyes. "I am not good at being a commoner, Jacob."

Looking at the lumpy oat flakes soup she'd made instead of the porridge he'd have liked to eat, he had to agree. He sighed.

"You know we can't go back. They made it clear that they don't want royals any longer, and I very much like being alive." He filled his bowl with the lumpy soup, put a generous helping of cream and sugar on it and sat beside her. "Also, I think that gardening is much more fun than ruling a kingdom."

"You know what I hate most?" Ruth pushed her half eaten soup aside and didn't wait for an answer. "As the sister of a gardener, I'll never get the chance to marry Prince Laurence."

Ah! That's how the land lies! Jacob smiled. "So they announced his return, did they?"

"Yesterday evening when you were already asleep," Ruth confirmed. "But he hasn't come here yet although he promised."

"Maybe he found the perfect bride after all."

"I am his perfect bride." She glared at him. "He said so."

"His parents would disagree. They want a royal princess for their son, and you know why we can't reveal ourselves." Jacob stood up, leaving his food behind. He had lost his appetite. Always, the arguments came back to this. "I'm in the herb garden for the afternoon, just in case you need me."

Jacob watched the kitchen maid who had collected the herbs he'd prepared for the cook return to the castle's side entrance. For a fleeting moment, he wished it were his sister on her way to work. If only she'd enjoy the simple things in life some more. A figure nodded to the maid and strode toward the herb garden. Recognizing Prince Laurence, Jacob turned away. He knew it wasn't possible to evade the prince, so he bent to remove some of the dried branches of the plant in front of him. When the prince arrived, Jacob straightened first and then bowed. "What can I do for you, your Majesty?"

"Stop calling me that, Jacob. We're friends, and I'm not king. May it remain that way for a long time yet." He sat on one of the knee-high decorative stones that marked the corners of the raised herb beds. "Is Ruth still in love with me?"

"Half the girls in town are in love with you, Laurence." Jacob hung his tools back onto their hooks on his belt and started walking toward the tool shed. "Why haven't you brought back a bride? Your parents must be upset."

"I know, but you should have seen the girls." Laurence hurried after him. "One tried to order me around as if I were a servant. Another one loved her gems more than anything. She barely even glanced at me. A third one clung to my arm as if she owned me, and yet another one had a voice like a rusty trumpet. The nicest princess I met on my travels was a seven year old, definitely too young."

Jacob stopped, turned, and looked Laurent into the eyes. "What do you want from me? I cannot change the fact that your parents won't accept a girl without blue blood, and I can't do magic."

"I want Ruth. I always did." Laurent's face contorted as if he was in pain. "I know she loves me too, and she'd do nicely as a princess. She knows most of what she needs to know already. Why can't we simply make up a story and pretend she's a princess? The way she's always keeping to the gardener's hut, it's not as if many people have seen her since you came here. No one would recognize her if we cheated a little. Please. You need to help us."

"There's nothing I can do." Jacob turned. "You'll have to let her go and find a bride your parents can live with. I need to water the lilies in the flower garden. Goodbye Laurence."

The prince sucked in a shuddering breath as if suppressing a sob. Jacob's heart contracted painfully. He hated to leave his friend behind like this. And he didn't like to see Ruth unhappy, but revealing their true identity was still too dangerous. Only this morning, he'd found a request in the papers seeking assistance in finding him and his sister. And if an article like that made it to the newspaper of an obscure kingdom like Laurence's, the revolution was still after them. He had to protect his sister even if it meant seeing her unhappy. He pressed his lips together and marched on.

Lightning and thunder came nearly at the same time. With his jacket over his head, Jacob hurried through the rain toward the little spot of light that must be the window of the gardener's house. Warmth and a hot tea was all he needed now. Maybe Ruth would be less sad, now that she'd seen Laurence again. A sudden wind ripped the door from his hand and slammed it against the wall. He needed all his strength to close it again. Only then did he notice that Ruth's cloak was missing. *She must be using it as a second cover*, he thought and went to the living room to build up a fire in the fireplace. Ruth wasn't there. He checked the kitchen, empty, and her bedroom; no one there either. Where was she? Frantically he searched his bedroom and the laundry room, even the attic, but found no sign of his sister. Had she gone out? In this weather? He had to find her. With trembling fingers, he donned the thick felt coat he had bought from a coach driver a little while back, grabbed the lantern that had guided him home from its hook near the window, and hurried out of the house again.

"Ruth!" He ran along the path to the castle. Maybe she had gone for a walk with Laurence and got lost in the thunderstorm on her way back. Jacob kept calling her name, but no one answered. The howling of the wind and the ear-splitting claps of thunder drowned out any other sound. The lantern's light blew out when he left the little artificial woods that surrounded the gardener's hut, but the lightning was bright and came often enough for him to see by.

He searched the gardens until his cloak was soaked. Tired, scared, and with a sore throat, he decided couldn't do it on his own. Surely Laurence would help him. A few minutes later, he stumbled into the castle's kitchen. To his surprise, several maids were busy, filling the big cauldron with water and preparing a light meal. He stood to the side, hung his coat beside the big, open fireplace, and watched the commotion. When the food had been taken away, he stopped one of the maids.

"Why are you still so busy? I thought everyone would be in bed at this time of night."

"We've got a visitor who is soaked the the skin, the poor girl." The maid laughed. "And with that kind of thunderstorm, most of us wouldn't have been able to sleep anyway."

"A girl?" Jacob bent forward. His heart thudded in his chest from a sudden worry. Had Ruth done something stupid?

"The prince insists she's a princess, although she never confirmed that." The maid wiped a strand of hair from her face. "His parents are skeptical. I mean why on earth would a princess walk through this kind of weather?"

Jacob leaned his back against the wall and closed his eyes. *Oh, Ruth, what have you done?* He tried not to be angry with her. She hadn't seen the revolutionaries kill their parents. After all, she'd been visiting the neighboring kingdom at the time. He had to get her out of this mess.

"Say…" The maid touched his arm. "Are you alright?"

Jacob opened his eyes and smiled at her. "Yes. Yes I am."

He waited until most servants had left the kitchen before he slipped into the long hall leading to the staircase that'd take him to the royal family's rooms. Laurence had smuggled him in a couple of times, so he knew how to find his friend's bedroom. Once there, he had to wait for quite a long time before the prince showed up.

Laurence's face lit up when he noticed Jacob. "I'm so glad you came." He hugged his friend for a moment.

Jacob fought the urge to slap him. He hissed, "Have you got the slightest idea what you did? This … this … folly might cost Ruth and my lives."

"Stop being so melodramatic. All Ruth and I want is to get married." Laurence sat on the side of his bed and sighed. "That's just proving to be more complicated than I thought."

"Your parents will not accept her unless she can prove she's a princess." Jacob smiled a grim smile. If the king and queen didn't approve of Ruth, they'd send her away soon and all would be well again.

"It's worse than that," Laurence said. "Father decided that if she can't prove that she's a princess, she'll get flogged, and Mother came up with the most ridiculous test ever."

Jacob's heart plummeted. Ruth wouldn't survive the kind of flogging Laurence's father liked to use as punishments. Whichever way he looked, they were in trouble. He needed to get Ruth out of the castle this very night. The faster, the further away they would be at daybreak.

"Aren't you going to ask me about the test then?" Laurent seemed surprised.

"I'm sure you're going to tell me anyway." Jacob was too tired to be friendly.

"Mother insists that Ruth sleeps on a tower of 25 mattresses. She'll hide a pea under the bottom one, and if Ruth feels it through all the cushioning, she'll convince Mother. And Father agreed to the test. The servants are already preparing the bed while Ruth is having a bath." Laurence grabbed his forehead with both hands. "Who has ever heard of something that silly."

Jacob swallowed his surprise. Ruth wouldn't need to tell them where she came from? Things might not be as bleak as he thought. If Laurence's parents accepted her as a daughter in law, she'd be safe from the revolutionaries, and he might be able to sneak back and find out what happened to his friends, his cousins, uncles, and aunts. For all he cared, the revolutionaries could keep the kingdom, but he wanted his family back. He cleared his throat. "How are they going to stop you from helping her? You could tell her about the pea, so she can lie to your parents."

Laurence shrugged. "I'm chaperoned at all times when she's around, and the minute she goes to bed, a soldier will watch the door to my room."

"In that case, I'd better leave you right now." Jacob smiled, and for the first time in years, he really felt a glimmer of hope in his heart. "Maybe things will turn out for the best after all. Which room did they put her in?"

The hopeful surprise on Laurence's face amused him as he hurried through the corridors to the castle's west wing where the guest rooms were. He arrived at the Blue Room as the last servant left. Hurriedly he hid in a niche behind a tapestry until the maid was gone. Then, he slipped into the darkened room.

His sister was still up, sitting beside the fireplace in a lace-nightgown. When she saw Jacob, she jumped up. "I'm not coming with you. The king agreed on testing me tomorrow. If he considers me to be a princess, Laurence will be allowed to marry me."

"You're wrong. The test is tonight. Luckily you bruise easily." He explained the test with the pea and his plan.

Ruth paled, but then her resolve visible hardened. She pressed her lips together and jutted her chin forward. "If that's what it takes to marry the love of my life, do it."

Jacob cupped her cheek with his hand. "I'll need to poke you several times throughout the night so the bruises have different colors. The king's not stupid, just ignorant of the way other people live." He turned to the bed and looked for the pea. The queen had put it at shoulder height, which was perfect for what he had to do. He turned to his sister. "Are you sure, you're up to it? It'll hurt somewhat."

Ruth nodded and began to climb the ladder that stood beside the wobbly tower. Jacob followed her with the poker from the fireplace in his hand.

When the first rays of the sun rose over the horizon, Ruth stretched. "I've never slept this bad. Do you think it'll work?"

Jacob glanced at the round bruises in different colors on her neck, decollete, and shoulders and nodded. "The shadows under your eyes will help too. Just play it save, will you?"

"Are you leaving?" Ruth sat up and grabbed his arm. "I can't do this without you."

"I have to leave. What do you think they'll do if they find a young man in the reputed princess' room? I'm sure they won't wait until I explain about our biological origins." He freed his arm and climbed down the ladder.

Ruth followed him.

After he'd put the stick back on the pile of kindling, she hugged him so tight, he could barely breathe. "I promise I'll never, ever tell anyone where I'm from. Not even Laurence. And that I have a brother will remain our secret."

"I'll visit as soon as I know what happened to the rest of our family." Jacob hugged her back, but more gentle. "I'll miss you. Give Laurence a big hug from me." He slipped from the room and hid in the same niche as the night before. Peeking through a gap between the tapestry and the wall allowed him to see the door to the Blue Room. He didn't have to wait long. Obviously curiosity had dragged the royals from their beds much earlier than usual. In their nightgowns, all three traipsed to Ruth's door.

Carefully the king opened it a crack. His eyebrows shot up and he looked at his wife, whispering, "She's not in her bed."

The queen opened the door wide and sailed past him toward Ruth. Her voice carried. "What's wrong, my dear. Is the bed not to your liking?"

"Oh no, everything is fine, your Majesty. I cannot complain." Ruth's voice sounded tired.

"Dear me!" The queen's voice rose a pitch. "You're covered in bruises."

"Well, there must have been a lump somewhere in my bed. It felt like a rock." Jacob could well imagine the apologetic face his sister used with these words.

"See, Harold, I told you she's a princess." The queen's words drew the king into the Blue Room. Only Laurence was still standing in the corridor. Jacob risked whistling. The prince half turned, and Jacob lifted the tapestry a little. His friend's smile looked so happy as if he'd received the most precious gift in the world – which, in a way, he had. Jacob waved a short farewell, and when Laurence entered Ruth's room too, he slipped away silently.

THE ORIGINAL: PUSS IN BOOTS

by Charles Perrault

There was a miller who left no more estate to the three sons he had than his mill, his ass, and his cat. The partition was soon made. Neither scrivener nor attorney was sent for. They would soon have eaten up all the poor patrimony. The eldest had the mill, the second the ass, and the youngest nothing but the cat. The poor young fellow was quite comfortless at having so poor a lot.

"My brothers," said he, "may get their living handsomely enough by joining their stocks together; but for my part, when I have eaten up my cat, and made me a muff of his skin, I must die of hunger."

The Cat, who heard all this, but made as if he did not, said to him with a grave and serious air: "Do not thus afflict yourself, my good master. You have nothing else to do but to give me a bag and get a pair of boots made for me that I may scamper through the dirt and the brambles, and you shall see that you have not so bad a portion in me as you imagine."

The Cat's master did not build very much upon what he said. He had often seen him play a great many cunning tricks to catch rats and mice, as when he used to hang by the heels, or hide himself in the meal, and make as if he were dead; so that he did not altogether despair of his affording him some help in his miserable condition. When the Cat had what he asked for he booted himself very gallantly, and putting his bag about his neck, he held the strings of it in his two forepaws and went into a warren where was great abundance of rabbits. He put bran and sow-thistle into his bag, and stretching out at length, as if he had been dead, he waited for some young rabbits, not yet acquainted with the deceits of the world, to come and rummage his bag for what he had put into it.

Scarce was he lain down but he had what he wanted. A rash and foolish young rabbit jumped into his bag, and Monsieur Puss, immediately drawing close the strings, took and killed him without pity. Proud of his prey, he went with it to the palace and asked to speak with his majesty. He was shown upstairs into the King's apartment, and, making a low reverence, said to him: "I have brought you, sir, a rabbit of the warren, which my noble lord the Marquis of Carabas" (for that was the title which puss was pleased to give his master) "has commanded me to present to your majesty from him."

"Tell thy master," said the king, "that I thank him and that he does me a great deal of pleasure."

Another time he went and hid himself among some standing corn, holding still his bag open, and when a brace of partridges ran into it he drew the strings and so caught them both. He went and made a present of these to the king, as he had done before of the rabbit which he took in the warren. The king, in like manner, received the partridges with great pleasure, and ordered him some money for drink.

The Cat continued for two or three months thus to carry his Majesty, from time to time, game of his master's taking. One day in particular, when he knew for certain that he was to take the air along the river-side, with his daughter, the most beautiful princess in the world, he said to his master: "If you will follow my advice your fortune is made. You have nothing else to do but go and wash yourself in the river, in that part I shall show you, and leave the rest to me."

The Marquis de Carabas did what the Cat advised him to, without knowing why or wherefore. While he was washing the King passed by, and the Cat began to cry out:

"Help! help! My Lord Marquis de Carabas is going to be drowned."

At this noise the King put his head out of the coach-window, and, finding it was the Cat who had so often brought him such good game, he commanded his guards to run immediately to the assistance of his Lordship the Marquis de Carabas. While they were drawing the poor Marquis out of the river, the Cat came up to the coach and told the King that, while his master was washing, there came by some rogues, who went off with his clothes, though he had cried out: "Thieves! thieves!" several times, as loud as he could.

This cunning Cat had hidden them under a great stone. The King immediately commanded the officers of his wardrobe to run and fetch one of his best suits for the Lord Marquis de Carabas.

The King caressed him after a very extraordinary manner, and as the fine clothes he had given him extremely set off his good mien (for he was well made and very handsome in his person), the King's daughter took a secret inclination to him, and the Marquis de Carabas had no sooner cast two or three respectful and somewhat tender glances but she fell in love with him to distraction. The King would needs have him come into the coach and take part of the airing. The Cat, quite overjoyed to see his project begin to succeed, marched on before, and, meeting with some countrymen, who were mowing a meadow, he said to them: "Good people, you who are mowing, if you do not tell the King that the meadow you mow belongs to my Lord Marquis of Carabas, you shall be chopped as small as herbs for the pot."

The King did not fail asking of the mowers to whom the meadow they were mowing belonged.

"To my Lord Marquis de Carabas," answered they altogether, for the Cat's threats had made them terribly afraid.

"You see, sir," said the Marquis, "this is a meadow which never fails to yield a plentiful harvest every year."

The Master Cat, who went still on before, met with some reapers, and said to them: "Good people, you who are reaping, if you do not tell the King that all this corn belongs to the Marquis de Carabas, you shall be chopped as small as herbs for the pot."

The King, who passed by a moment after, would needs know to whom all that corn, which he then saw, did belong.

"To my Lord Marquis de Carabas," replied the reapers, and the King was very well pleased with it, as well as the Marquis, whom he congratulated thereupon. The Master Cat, who went always before, said the same words to all he met, and the King was astonished at the vast estates of my Lord Marquis de Carabas.

Monsieur Puss came at last to a stately castle, the master of which was an ogre, the richest had ever been known; for all the lands which the King had then gone over belonged to this castle. The Cat, who had taken care to inform himself who this ogre was and what he could do, asked to speak with him, saying he could not pass so near his castle without having the honor of paying his respects to him.

The ogre received him as civilly as an ogre could do, and made him sit down.

"I have been assured," said the Cat, "that you have the gift of being able to change yourself into all sorts of creatures you have a mind to; you can, for example, transform yourself into a lion, or elephant, and the like."

"That is true," answered the ogre very briskly; "and to convince you, you shall see me now become a lion."

Puss was so sadly terrified at the sight of a lion so near him that he immediately got into the gutter, not without abundance of trouble and danger, because of his boots, which were of no use at all to him in walking upon the tiles. A little while after, when Puss saw that the ogre had resumed his natural form, he came down, and owned he had been very much frightened.

"I have been, moreover, informed," said the Cat, "but I know not how to believe it, that you have also the power to take on you the shape of the smallest animals; for example, to change yourself into a rat or a mouse; but I must own to you I take this to be impossible."

"Impossible!" cried the ogre; "you shall see that presently."

And at the same time he changed himself into a mouse, and began to run about the floor. Puss no sooner perceived this but he fell upon him and ate him up.

Meanwhile the King, who saw, as he passed, this fine castle of the ogre's, had a mind to go into it. Puss, who heard the noise of his Majesty's coach running over the draw-bridge, ran out, and said to the King:

"Your Majesty is welcome to this castle of my Lord Marquis de Carabas."

"What! my Lord Marquis," cried the King, "and does this castle also belong to you? There can be nothing finer than this court and all the stately buildings which surround it; let us go into it, if you please."

The Marquis gave his hand to the Princess, and followed the King, who went first. They passed into a spacious hall, where they found a magnificent collation, which the ogre had prepared for his friends, who were that very day to visit him, but dared not to enter, knowing the King was there. His Majesty was perfectly charmed with the good qualities of my Lord Marquis de Carabas, as was his daughter, who had fallen violently in love with him, and, seeing the vast estate he possessed, said to him, after having drunk five or six glasses: "It will be owing to yourself only, my Lord Marquis, if you are not my son-in-law."

The Marquis, making several low bows, accepted the honor which his Majesty conferred upon him, and forthwith, that very same day, married the Princess.

Puss became a great lord, and never ran after mice any more but only for his diversion.

THE DWARF AND THE TWINS
SNOW WHITE AND ROSE RED
Treasures Retold 1

Once upon a time in a world where magic and technology collide with unexpected consequences…

When Martin helps a pregnant woman to flee from the king's men, he doesn't know that the twins she bears will change his solitary life forever.

What if the Brother's Grimm misunderstood the dwarf in the original tale of "Snow White and Rose Red"?

The book includes a bonus story and the original fairy tale.

ISBN 978-3-95681-028-2
also available as eBook

Leave your eMail address so I can inform you about new releases, and this book will arrive as an eBook in your Inbox shortly after

http://www.katharinagerlach.com/readers

The Interview
The Devil with the Three Golden Hairs
Treasures Retold 11

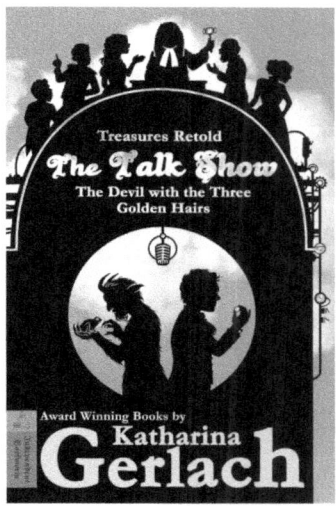

Once upon a time in a world where magic and technology collide with unexpected consequences…

The moderator only wants a good story, but the devil needs to get his magical hairs back or he and his grandmother will starve. However, is a talk-show really the right place to demand justice?

What if the Brother's Grimm hadn't known that „The Devil with the Three Golden Hairs" had good reasons for what he did?

The book includes a bonus story and the original fairy tale.

ISBN 978-3-95681-118-0
also available as eBook

www.ingramcontent.com/pod-product-compliance
Lightning Source LLC
Chambersburg PA
CBHW060941120626
46557CB00003B/1090